Big Tent Books

115 Bluebill Drive
Savannah, GA 31419
United States

Published with the assistance of the
helpful folks at DragonPencil.com

Kimberly Dawn Neumann -
Content Editor

Jodi Buckley -
Graphic Editor and
Digital Production Director

First Edition 2012
Printed and Bound in the U.S.A.

GINGERTOWN

THE JULIE NEEDLES WINTER WISH ADVENTURE

Written and Illustrated by DAVID GILLAM

Chapter One: The Needles' Farm

The smoke of toasted pines filled the air, for inside, Ida Mae Needles cozied up her little shop with an old iron stove. All who entered this place of business found their senses tantalized not only by the smoky kindling, but also by the fresh baked aroma of gingerbread treats: gingerbread men, gingerbread cakes, gingerbread muffins, gingerbread houses, gingerbread dogs, gingerbread birds, gingerbread cats and gingerbread girls with pink icing curls. Ida Mae's selection was beyond compare.

"One for you, one for you, and one for you." Ida Mae handed a cookie to each eager child. All three were full of smiles.

Chomp! In unison, all three heads of all three cookies were bitten off.

A stern father figure felt he just had to speak up, "You children save the sweets for the ride home," as the mother guided her family out of the shop.

"Thank you. Happy holidays! And remember, corn season starts in August." Ida Mae waved at the family as they drove off with their hand cut tree tied to the top of their station wagon.

What a happy sight, thought Ida Mae, peeking out of the bakeshop's front window. *They even had their dog in the back.*

"Your ginger treats are as beautiful as ever. Oh I wish I had your patience for baking." It was Redda Pinesky, one of Ida Mae's oldest acquaintances. Taking a quick handful of cookie samples from the small display basket, Redda continued while licking the sugar frosting off of her fingertips.

"I… love… these… mmm, and so will my family. Do me a favor, Ida sweetie. Put a couple more of the spicy snap cookies in a separate little bag. Those will be my little travel snacks for the way home." This very adult woman then giggled like a child in anticipation of the secret cookies she was about to enjoy. Redda had a plump round figure. Sweets were her passion and she made no excuses for loving them.

"Ida," commented Redda, glancing over at the bakeshop's bulletin board, "You never got one of my pink printouts, did you?" In her hand, Redda was holding a stack of pink flyers. Redda was active in many of the local social events. Even though she hadn't officially been appointed the town's event planner, she felt as though she had.

"If I did, I never had a chance to read it. What are you planning this time?" asked Ida Mae.

"What am I planning? Why, it's the big Christmas Eve Gala. It's been all the talk of the town. Don't you read your Buzzin' Bee Gazette?"

Ida Mae's look of not knowing or remembering was due to the shop's hectic schedule during the holidays.

"Oh Ida, you have to take a little time for yourself now and then." In her own way Redda meant well but in that same way she also couldn't control her little jabs. "We're not young girls anymore."

Redda's loud, colorful ensemble – a hand-crocheted afghan and matching winter beret accented with a pair of fuzzy high-heeled winter boots – was very fitting for this town busybody. In contrast, Ida Mae was the picture of a modest countrywoman in her simple oversized cardigan, which she layered over a comfy cotton blue sweater. Her only little extra for the holidays was a single jingle-bell lapel pin. The distinct difference between their fashion choices presented no real problem, however. It was more a welcome variation of personalities.

"So, are you coming to the Gala tonight?" quizzed Redda again.

"Oh, that depends on a lot of things. You know Redda, sometimes I'm busy here right up until the very last minute."

"Well, give my love to Joe, and oh, to your grandchildren. I heard they're staying with you for the holidays. Bye now." And off Redda went with her bags of fresh baked goods.

It was the end of a long day, and contrary to Redda's observation that she needed to take a break now and then Ida Mae enjoyed all the work. She had been doing it for more years than she could remember. But today is over, and it was finally time to close up the shop. Standing outside, she saw the approaching storm in the distance. It was also time to locate her grandchildren.

"Jodi! Julie! Brian! Time to come in for dinner." *Ching, ching, ching, ching, ching, ching, ching, ching.* She shook a cluster of sleigh bells that hung on the post in front of the shop. From out of nowhere, a purring gray tiger-striped cat buzzed around her feet.

"Meow."

4

"Tiger Lily! And where have you been hiding? I know. You're hungry." Ida Mae removed the "Open" sign from the bakeshop window and replaced it with "See You Soon."

"Go find the kids, Tiger Lily." Most people say cats can't be trained. Ida Mae knew better. The cat answered, "Meow," and off she darted into the snowy landscape.

Walking up the hill to the main house, carrying a basket of items and shaking sleigh bells, Ida Mae was joined by her husband, Joe Needles. The dark clouds in the distance were creeping closer and closer.

Racing from tree to tree, zigging and zagging between small shrubs and leafless undergrowth, Tiger Lily was greeted by her many friends. The squirrels shook their tails, the snow bunnies wiggled their noses, and, dusting off the fresh falling snow, a large owl shook its feathers. Aware of the approaching storm, all the little creatures appeared to be guiding the oversized farm cat through the maze of undergrowth. In one acrobatic cat-leap, she sprang up and onto a tree branch.

"Tiger Lily!" Brian was happily surprised. Up in the low-growing tree, Brian, a seven-year-old boy was doing what he did best - being Brian. He jumped down into a snowdrift. "Co'mon Tiger Lily!" Following behind, the adventurous cat jumped too. Off they went, running through the Needles' farm. They raced past the snow-covered rose garden, and wound through the old-fashioned trellis archways as they headed towards the many rows of cultivated spruces, firs, white pines, scotch pines and balsas.

Pointing to a particular tree, Julie Needles, Brian's bigger sister, had made a decision. "This one. This is the one I want."

Standing next to Julie and holding the saw was Jodi. She was the oldest of the three. To any passerby, it was quite apparent that these two were sisters. They both had long curly brown hair and dark hazel eyes, a family trait they got from their grandmother, Ida Mae. "Are you absolutely, positively convinced that this is the one already?" Jodi was losing her patience. Julie had lead them all over the farm to find just the right tree.

"Ye-ess, I am absolutely positively convinced, totally sure, already, that this is the one I want.," mimicked Julie in a slightly agitated way.

"Good," sighed Jodi, "Because… we've been through this everyday for about a week now. I cut it down and after we drag it back to the house you suddenly declare, 'I must have a more perfect tree to decorate.' Then we drag it to the roadside stand for some- body else to buy and the next day I'm out here again with Little-Miss-Can't-Make-Up- Her-Picky-Mind."

"Mommy and Daddy said that I could pick out the tree this year, and Gramma and Grampa said I could too. It's my decision," said Julie.

"A tree. Not the entire forest. Do you have any idea how long it took for this tree to get this big? Jodi smiled at the evergreen they were standing in front of with apprecia- tion. "Just look at this beautiful, silent, green, friend-to-the-planet earth. This oxygen- making, shade-providing, small animal and bird sheltering tree had to be nurtured and hand-planted and fertilized and debugged and clipped. It had to fight the hard winters and hot, dry summers. It's probably older than both of us put together, and in the blink of a saw blade it'll be dragged off for firewood when you can't make up your finicky little decorator mind."

Jodi's feelings about the beauty that nature provided ran deep. She had no prob- lem sharing her values with her family. Because of her grandparents and her upbringing, she completely understood and respected the cycle of tree farming. But with her newly developed educational point of view, there were never enough opportunities for her to enlighten her little sister as to her opinions on botanical ethics. "I love having an old-fash- ioned Christmas, but if I had my way there'd be a law making artificial trees mandatory."

"Grampa says getting people to give up the sweet fresh smell of pinesap is about as easy getting hit by lightning twice in one day." Julie pulled a fresh soft-needled balsa branch up to her nose to sniff. "Besides, it makes me happy."

"If we're going to harvest them just when they're ready to shoot up into majestic giants, then the very least we can do is have a little respect for the life these living green creatures have on this planet. They're not just trees. They're our friends. And I believe that trees have feelings, too."

"Do snowflakes have feelings?" goaded Julie.

Ignoring her childish comment, Jodi pressed on. "Years ago a scientific study con- cerning the life cycle of plants was conducted. One plant was forced to listen to loud, angry music all its life, while the other was treated to the soothing sounds of classical music. Now which one do you think grew bigger and faster?"

"The one with the most fertilizer?" wisecracked Julie.

"No, the one with the happier vibrations. And if plants can sense music, that must mean that they have feelings too."

"I know," commented Julie. "You tell me every time we cut down a tree."

Julie enjoyed the predictable speeches her sister made. It was fun to see her get so emotional about her "current teenage cause." That's what her mother, father, and grandparents secretly called it out of the earshot of Jodi, so as not to upset her. And Julie, being the attentive little listener in the family, had overheard all the private conversations on this matter… as well as many others.

And quite frankly, this was most likely the real reason that Julie didn't want to make up her mind so quickly. The picky, can't-make-up-her-mind little sister enjoyed watching Jodi get all worked up about it. Imitating her older sister, Julie continued to recite what she had heard for the last nine days. "Trees are like people, with their own individual personalities. And if you look closely you can see a different face in each one."

"I can't believe it. Am I finally getting through to you?" Jodi was in awe. Her teachings had stuck… or at least the words had. "Look at this one." Jodi stepped back to get a feeling about who it resembled. "Quick! Who does it look like?"

"A big green tree ready to be cut down and covered with lights," smirked Julie.

Undaunted, Jodi continued concentrating on the tree. "I see… a clown lady! In a circus. Licking a sucker while wearing a pointy witches' hat."

"And that one?" Even though Julie couldn't see what Jodi was able to see, she still wanted to hear her sister's incredible descriptions.

"Daddy standing in front of the refrigerator eating ice cream right out of the carton."

Julie laughed. Their father was a hefty man who enjoyed indulging his late-night craving for sweets.

Playing along, Julie decided to join in the fun. "This one looks like the school lunch lady, wearing a hairnet and holding a spatula. She imitated the lunch lady, putting her hands on her hips. "You kids are just out of control today. Why can't we have a quiet peaceful meal for a change?"

Jodi stood holding the saw ready to cut. "Well which one is it, little sister? This is your last pick."

Julie thought for a moment. She looked back and forth. "Hmmm… the Clown-Lady-In-The-Circus-Licking-A-Sucker-Wearing-A-Pointy-Witches'-Hat tree."

Jodi knelt down in the snow at the base of the tree. "Hold up the branches so I can reach the trunk with the saw."

Julie did as requested. *Ssssssss… huh… sssss… huh… sss… huh… sss… huh…* The trunk of the tree was being cut by Jodi's strong arm. Then she stopped for a moment. She lifted her head. "I hear something. Listen… bells."

"It's Gramma. She wants us to come help frost cookies for the gift booties after dinner, remember?"

Another wonderful thing about Ida Mae was that each year, even with having to run the busy little roadside bakeshop, she still found time to make gift booties for all of her friends and family. Gift booties were her own special version of fireplace stockings.

"I hate those commercial creations on the store shelves," she'd say. "They don't even look like real feet. Maybe a dinosaur could stick its foot inside, but not a regular little girl or boy. The booties I make look like real boots…that real feet could go into."

After having made her observations on store-bought stockings known to many a might-as-well-be-deaf local shopkeeper, Ida Mae had long since decided to make her own. Starting in July of each year, she'd assemble piles of fabric remnants. Each week she'd sew a couple. By the time Christmas arrived, the pile of gift booties sitting on her dining room table were ready to be filled. Ida Mae's famous gingerbread goodies needed to be frosted and wrapped, and then put into the bootie sacks. Jodi and Julie had promised to help this year.

Sssss… huh… sss… huh… sss… Thunk! The tree fell over, ready to be pulled to the Needles' big farmhouse. The joyful glee of the season filled Julie. "I can't wait to decorate it." Tiger Lily suddenly ran to the girls. Julie picked her up and cradled her. "Tiger Lily! And what do you want for Christmas, little girl?"

"Meow."

"A pet angelfish?" Even though Tiger Lily was Ida Mae's happy farm cat, Julie treated Tiger Lily as though she were her own little baby. The cat loved it.

"Meow."

"Oh you wanted a baked angelfish rolled in catnip…"

"Meow."

"…with cheddar cheese sprinkles?"

Julie put the cat down and ran towards a big snow pile. She jumped in, covering her entire body. Then she rolled on the ground, positioning herself to make a snow angel. She had mixed emotions. "Lucky us, cutting trees and frosting cookies while Mommy and Daddy get to sail with Uncle Peter on a cruise ship to Venezuela for two weeks. It's not fair! I wanted to go with them."

Jodi had her own views. "Well, I love it here at Gramma and Grampa's farm.   It's quiet…"

"We've been here without cable television for nine whole days," whined Julie.

"Who needs cable? It's the perfect place for me to study for my college prep ex-ams," stated Jodi.

"Whatever," remarked Julie. "With no computer to glue yourself to, you'll probably have a nervous breakdown."

"Have you ever heard of something called books? Ya know, the kind you don't color in?"

"Books are made from trees, ya know." Julie just loved getting one up on Jodi.

Even though the Needles family was very close, the kind of close where Gramma and Grampa were as much a part of their grandchildren's lives as their parents were, this was the first Christmas that the children had spent on the farm without their mother and father.

While lying in the snow looking up at the big wintry sky, Julie continued to speak her thoughts aloud to Jodi. "Mommy and Daddy are probably swimming in the ship's pool right now, while we're up here freezing and with nothing to do."

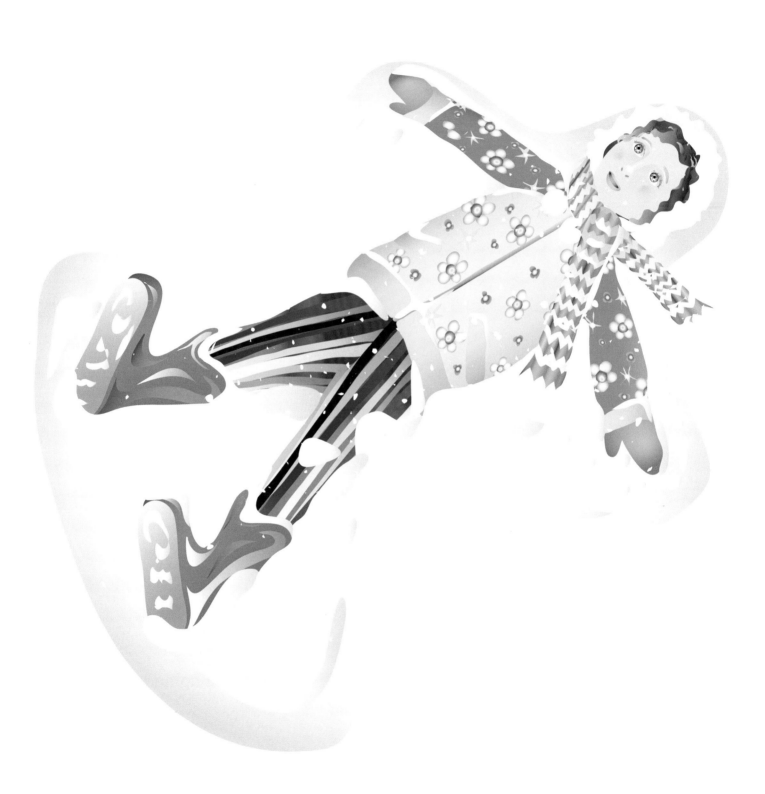

The separation, though it seemed not to have been a problem at first, was beginning to bother Julie, as was apparent through her constant acting-out. Jodi was aware of this, but quietly dismissed it.

"And where would you rather be on Christmas vacation? At the mall, scouting out all the plastic toys you think you need, and driving everybody crazy making your gift list even longer?" said Jodi.

Julie, lifting her head up and out of the snow declared, "Been there, done that. I just want all the presents that Daddy promised he'd get me."

"And in about eight or nine months, every one of them will be tossed in the 'I'm-tired-of-my-new-toys pile' and you'll want new ones. I think an old-fashioned Christmas will do you some good. A little less emphasis on the material and a lot more emphasis on substance."

"Everything that's older than me *is* old-fashioned for me. Right? And if that's true, then plastic toys and shopping in department stores are as special as sleigh bells and eggnog… for me." Julie's nine-year-old logic made sense somehow and even though Jodi didn't agree, she was impressed with her younger sister's debating skills. "Point well made, little sister."

Smack!

A snowball hit Jodi in the shoulder. Giggling could be heard from behind the shrubs. Jodi didn't have to guess. She knew there could be only one suspect.

"Brian!"

Suddenly and without warning, Julie jumped straight up out of the snow and onto her feet.

"I almost forgot!" And off she ran.

"Where are you going?" yelled Jodi after her.

The echo of Julie's voice faded along the long, tree-lined path.

My penny!

The end of Chapter One

Chapter Two: The Well in the Grove

Traveling farther into the enchanted wintry world of the Needles' farm, Julie headed for her favorite spot. Jodi knew just where she was off to, and followed behind, carrying Tiger Lily. It was a pretty little grove of age-old hemlock trees, trees that had never been cut. In the center of the grove stood a classic fieldstone water well with a bucket and a crank. Over the top of it was a small roof.

With her cheeks flushed red, and out of breath from running in the cold snowy weather, Julie panted, "I… have to… make a wish… with my lucky penny."

"You… and that… stupid penny." Jodi was also out of breath from chasing after her. "We've been hearing about it all day."

"Well, I only found this very lucky penny today."

Less winded now, Jodi asked, "Where did it come from, anyway?"

"It was stuck to an old piece of chewing gum on the back of Grampa's rusty old pickup truck."

"Ooo gross. Did you put the gum in your mouth?" asked Jodi.

"Nooo! Grampa said he got it from a carnival clown when he was a boy about my age."

Joe Needles was a quiet country man of little conversation. So when he shared his tale with Julie she paid strict attention to every detail. Grampa Joe's descriptive image of the carnival clown was as clear as if it were yesterday.

Julie retold the story to Jodi practically word for word, as she was an attentive listener. "Grampa said, growing up in the country, there wasn't all that much to look forward to in the summer. So when the traveling carnival came to town, everybody went. He said it was real exciting for farm children with no television. And did you know when Grampa was little, everybody called him Little Joe Needles?"

"Stick to the penny story. We don't have all night," chattered Jodi with nearly frozen teeth.

Julie made a face at Jodi and then continued. "So, anyway, Grampa piled into the back of Great Grampa Needles' truck with the rest of the family. When they got to the carnival, his brothers and sisters all ran off. Grampa was the last to leave the truck, and he promised not to get into any trouble. The sideshows were his favorite. The carnival barkers would always shout about all the weird things inside the tents that you could see for only a quarter. So when Grampa was walking through the crowds, looking at all the teaser acts on the platforms, he forgot to look where he was going and he tripped and fell right into the path of a very scary looking sideshow circus clown.

"The clown picked him up and brushed him off and said, 'It's real easy to get trampled by too much fun here at the carnival.'" Julie, always the dramatic one, added even more drama to her tale by speaking in the spooky voice she imagined the carnival clown had. "'But I like to think that you, my lucky little fellow, just stumbled onto the path of good fortune. Do you know what I have for you here?' And then from inside his pocket he took out a coin and showed it to Grampa. 'It's very, very old, and very lucky. And it's time for me to pass the good fortune it has brought me on to you.'"

Getting carried away with the story telling, Julie began to act out the tale like it was a school play. She imitated the way that she though Little Joe Needles might have responded upon hearing the carnival clown's words. "'Really? Wow!' Then the clown put the coin into Grampa's hand, and before the clown took his own hand away, he spoke… what did Grampa call it? Oh, yeah… 'Words of carnival wisdom.'"

Growing even more animated, Julie continued in an over-mysterious adult voice. "'This is a magic penny. Not just any throw-it-down-the-well-and-wish-for-chickens-to-lay-fresh-eggs-in-the-morning penny, but a penny that can make your sleepy dreams come true. So be careful how you use it, and what you dream about, or you might wake up… a duck! Quack, quack, quack, quack, quack, quack, quack!'"

Julie finished explaining, "Then the clown laughed and gave Grampa a goofy but scary smile with his painted face. Grampa wanted to go on the rides, but he had a hole in his pocket. He didn't want to lose the magic penny, so he went back to the truck, took the gum out of his mouth, rolled the penny in it, stuck it under the back fender and forgot all about it... until today."

Jodi listened, but still had more questions. "So how did you get it?"

"While I was kicking snow off the truck fenders behind the barn, the penny fell off. So now it's mine." Julie held it up proudly for Jodi to see.

Up close, it really didn't look like a penny. It wasn't copper, but was a silver color. It was like no coin Jodi had ever seen before. "This looks like some kind of token from an arcade. I don't even think it's real."

"It is too real." Julie pulled it back into her tight grip.

"What are you going to wish for?" Jodi loved teasing Julie. "Your very own pull up diapers?"

"Nooo."

Brian, covered in frosty white bliss, popped his head out from behind a snow bank. "How about a baby rattle?"

Julie, being the middle child, got it from both ends. Brian, not wanting to be the youngest, instigated at every opportunity.

"I'm Julie. I'm a big baby," continued Brian, goading his sister.

"You're the baby," retorted Julie.

"Goo goo, ga ga, where's my bottle, where's my hair brush, I want new tap shoes. Waaa, tap, tap, tap, tap…" Brian slipped back into hiding.

"Very funny Brian. I plan to wish for something much more adult."

Before Julie could continue her thought, Jodi finished it for her. "A Talking Teresa doll with glowing neon fiber-optic hair and a metallic glow-in-the-dark party dress."

Julie deflated, "You know my wish."

"Big surprise! You've been whining about Talking Teresa since June. And with your choice of wardrobe, I am confident that neither you nor that stupid doll will ever get lost in the forest."

Jodi was referring to Julie's multi-bright, mix-and-nothing-matches attire.

Julie's boots were bright rubber-pink and she had on multicolored, striped corduroys. Her authentic 60s floral-patterned jacket had been her Mom's and therefore she felt compelled to wear it… all the time. Add to that the mismatched mittens, hat and scarf compliments of Gramma's trip to the Goodwill and it was clear that Julie was definitely one little girl who wasn't swayed by conventional clothing tastes. Not seeing her fashion sense as bizarre or daring, Julie reminded her big sister that one day she would be a famous fashion designer.

"Tap!" Brian needed to keep his presence known.

"Oh, just give me the penny," said Jodi. "I'll make a wish worth making."

"Like what?" Julie wanted to know.

"Tap! Tap!" Brian was still aching for attention.

Jodi had no trouble thinking of the perfect gift for herself. "A pair of Noise Blaster ear muffs." Being the oldest had its advantages and its disadvantages. The main disadvantage was having to listen to Brian and Julie fight all the time.

"Tap! Tap! Tap!"

"Someday I'll also be a huge tap dance star," declared Julie.

"Tap! Tap! Tap! Tap!" Brian's relentless peskiness was starting to get to Julie.

"…who wears the most fan-ta-bu-lous…"

"Tap! Tap!"

"…fashions…"

"Tap! Tap!"

"…ever!"

"Tap!!!"

Julie's blood began to get hotter. Brian had a way of pushing all her buttons at once.

Jodi was growing impatient. "Just toss the stupid penny. It's getting colder and Gramma's waiting. I can hear the bells again. Listen…"

"I can't just toss it in the well like I'm throwing out the garbage."

Jodi, who was a budding high school psychologist, had a few words of wisdom to impart to Julie. At this point, she would have said anything to help get this wishing-well ritual over with. "You have to close your eyes and believe it. See it. Materialize it."

Making a firm choice was always a weak point for Julie. "One coin, one wish. One well. One special gift." She held the coin up and concentrated. "I'm seeing. I'm believing. I'm ready… Aaugh!"

From behind Julie, moving like the seven-year-old trouble-making lightning bolt he was, Brian snatched the sacred coin from Julie's hand.

"Yeow!" Even Tiger Lily jumped at this unexpected move.

"Brian! That's my penny!"

"No it's my penny. 'Cause you owe me money from when I gave you a nickel."

"You never gave me a nickel," screamed Julie.

"Uh huh… last summer when we went to Thunder Park… so it's mine."

Before Brian knew it, Jodi snatched the penny out of his hand. "I believe this penny is technically mine because I gave Brian five dollars to buy hot dogs on that same day last summer at Thunder Park, and I never got my change back."

Jodi couldn't resist getting in on the fun. "Oh what will I wish for?" Pointing her finger at Brian in a playful manner, Jodi pretended she had magic powers. "Zap! You're a chicken."

Down on his knees and flapping his elbows, Brian played along. "Cluck. Cluck, Cluck."

"Zap! You're a piggy."

Responding to Jodi's magic finger game, Brian was instantly on all fours. "Oink, Oink, Oink."

Enraged, Julie jumped up, trying with all her might to get the penny. Jodi, being a bit quicker than her nine-year-old sister, held tight. Julie fell on Brian, and a rolling-around-in-the-snow wrestling match of angry sister versus bratty brother ensued. Pushing snow in Brian's face, Julie shouted, "I wish you were a toad with lots of warts."

"You already are," Brian giggled.

Julie pulled Brian's hat over his face. "With pickled green skin… to match the boogers up your nose."

"You're a booger." Brian managed to roll the two of them over. He was on top now.

The breaking point had been reached. "I hate you, you little snotweed!" shouted Julie, rolling the two of them over again. Brian flipped himself onto his stomach, so Julie pushed his face into the snow. It was hard to tell if he was laughing or crying. He thoroughly enjoyed this kind of roughhousing.

When Jodi got between them in order to break it up, Julie seized the opportunity to retrieve her penny. In spite of her reclaimed victory, Julie was still visibly upset. "I wish I didn't have to listen to you always telling me what to do!"

"News flash, little sister. This is my purpose on the planet… being your boss."

Brian, seeking more physical confrontation, continued to goad Julie. "I wish you were a tree, so I could chop you down and turn you into a picnic table."

Julie responded with a tight-lipped stare. "If you were a tree I'd turn you into a toilet seat."

"You smell like one," snarled Brian.

Jodi had had enough. "I wish the both of you were trees, so I wouldn't have to listen to you two fighting all the time."

Aiming with all his might, Brian shot forward like a bullet out of a gun, butting Julie's stomach with his head. Losing her balance, she screamed.

The penny was once again in Brian's hand. He stood next to the well and held the penny over the opening, pretending he might drop it in. This was the last straw for Julie. She charged at him like bull. He stood face-to-face with her, mugging a full-cheeked smile. In an eye-squinting, lip-biting moment, Julie lifted her hand and… *Smack!*

She slapped him across his smug little face. With the shock of being struck, Brian let go of the penny.

Julie felt time slowing down as she watched the carnival treasure spin downward into the deep well. Afraid to look, while at the same time dying to see, Brian, Jodi, and Tiger Lily joined Julie, all of them leaning over, peering down into the dark expanse of the circular stone shaft.

The end of Chapter Two

Chapter Three: The Approaching Storm

"Aughhh!" Frustration and rage screamed out of Julie, as she realized that what had just happened was real. Brian ran off laughing, of course.

"Now I won't get my special Christmas Eve wish. Why do I have to be in this stupid family at this stupid farm with nothing but stupid trees, trees, and more trees? Gramma and Grampa had to get Mommy and Daddy a stupid no-kids-cruise for Christmas. 'We'll have more fun here.' Well it's not fun here!"

"Well, Mom and Dad wouldn't need a no-kids vacation if you and Brian could stop fighting for two seconds." Jodi stopped for a burning moment to clear the accumulating fresh snowfall off the front of her eyeglasses. She put them back on with a focused stare towards her angry little sister.

Trying to further inflate an already tense situation, Julie persisted, "It's not just Brian and me. What about you and your stupid teenage cause. 'Save the trees! Save the trees!'"

"Don't press your luck little sister, or you may live to regret it."

Jodi, even though she really wanted to blast her little pressure cooker sister with a face full of snow, was now trying to be the calm adult. Biting her tongue, she continued to look down into the well with Tiger Lily.

Not satisfied with what she could see through the well's darkness, Jodi pulled a flashlight out of her shoulder tool bag. "Frozen stone... a frozen bucket... and... I think I can see it!"

"Meow?"

Julie leaned even farther over the edge. What she and her sister saw was unexpected. The precious wishing coin was lying on top of the ice at the bottom of the well.

"You're lucky," said Jodi. "The water is frozen."

"Maybe we can find a way to get my penny back before the ice melts. I know! We can put Tiger Lily in the bucket and lower her down to get it," shouted Julie with new-found optimism.

"Meow?"

"We can't do anything now, Julie. It's getting dark and a big storm is coming this way. Maybe tomorrow we can think of something."

Feeling like she'd just lost her best friend, Julie moped all the way back to the big farmhouse on the hill. First she told her grandmother what happened and Gramma Needles gave her a hot, fresh-out-of-the-oven gingerbread cookie to cheer her up. It didn't work.

Then she told Grampa Joe. He put her on his lap and hugged her for a while. It helped a little, but she was still sad.

After dinner, after frosting cookies, stuffing booties and watching a little TV, it was time to finally decorate the tree that Julie had taken so long to select.

"Grampa, I have too many orange ones in a row on this one." Brian was testing the old screw-in lights. He liked to mix up the colors in the process.

"Here you go." Grampa handed Brian a large tin coffee can full of extra bulbs. Then he slid himself under the tree to adjust the stand.

Brian had several strands of lights stretched over the sofa and end tables. "I'm ready. Plug 'em in again."

Gramma, who was seated on the floor next to the electrical wall socket, was thumbing through old Christmas cards. With Brian's signal she inserted the plug.

"They're all good Gramma." A warm multicolored glow reflected off Brian's happy face. "Yea!"

Gramma then unplugged the many sets, they were ready to be placed on the tree.

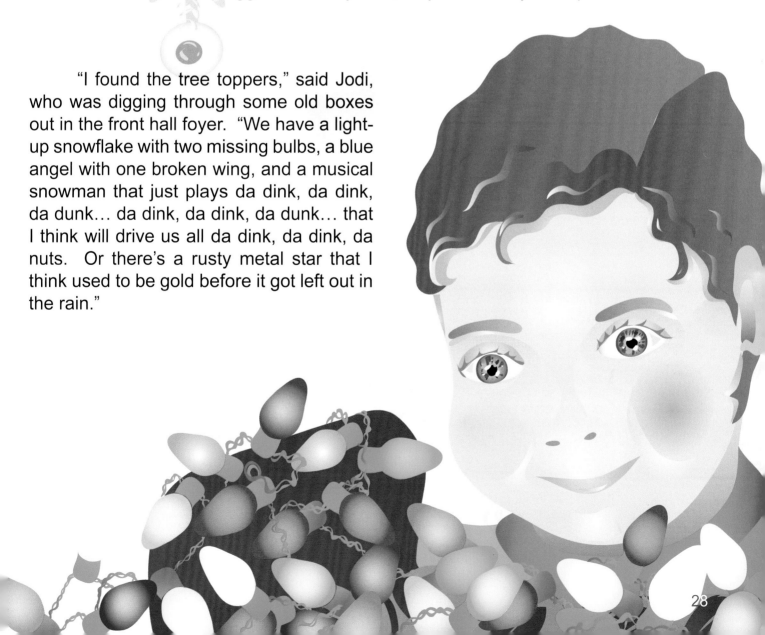

"I found the tree toppers," said Jodi, who was digging through some old boxes out in the front hall foyer. "We have a light-up snowflake with two missing bulbs, a blue angel with one broken wing, and a musical snowman that just plays da dink, da dink, da dunk… da dink, da dink, da dunk… that I think will drive us all da dink, da dink, da nuts. Or there's a rusty metal star that I think used to be gold before it got left out in the rain."

Before anyone could respond, Julie entered the front parlor with two big black plastic lawn and garden bags. Each was full of her lightweight creations.

"It's going to be a pink angel with silver glitter. I made her a new dress, and I can fix her wing. And we're not gonna use multicolored lights. I want all red and white bulbs."

"Oh no, The Fat-Hippo-Eating-A-Carton-Of-Macaroni is gonna be a stupid girls' tree!" exclaimed Brian.

"The Clown- Lady- In – The - Circus - Licking - A - Sucker - Wearing - A – Pointy - Witches'- Hat is my tree. I'm going to decorate it the way I want. And if this is a girls' tree we won't be needing these." In a snobbish, little girl snoot, Julie picked up the three small action figures that Brian had tied ribbons to and tossed them into an old shoebox. "Why don't you hang them on the closet door-knob. Upstairs. In your little boys' room."

"Gramma!" Brian was so upset he was ready to cry, but he held it in. Breathing heavily he picked up the little box and ran up to his room.

Julie yelled up the stairs at him. "Now look who's the baby. 'I'm gonna hang my stupid toys on the tree. Waah! Where's my rattle?'"

Julie turned toward the living room to see that Jodi, Gramma and Grampa were all staring at her in silent disappointment. Without a moment's regret for her territorial aggressiveness, she continued, not missing a beat. "I made white paper snowflakes and pink tissue paper carnations." She dumped out both bags onto the floor next to Gramma. "And we'll have tinsel and ginger-bread cookies on the tree this year."

Jodi, who now was nearly speechless, pointed a disapproving finger. "So that's where my twenty-four pound bright-white premium inkjet printer-paper went." She picked up a clipped and snipped paper snowflake from the huge pile and looked through it. The fact that it was pretty just made her all the madder. "You are such a little brat."

Julie, unwilling to back down, smiled at Jodi with the smug expression of victory. "It's my tree this year."

Jodi, who had enough, decided to go upstairs to check on Brian.

This all came to a halt when Ida Mae spoke up.

"Julie, I know you had a hard day today, but your spoiled, pouty behavior has run its course young lady. Trust me when I tell you that you have to let go of this penny thing now, or you are going to ruin Christmas for the entire family."

"I'm not ruining Christmas, Brian and Jodi ruined Christmas, and you and Grampa did, too."

"We did? How did we ruin your Christmas?" Ida Mae and Joe were at a loss. After all, they had indulged her every whim from the moment she'd arrived.

"Cause I'm here and Mommy and Daddy are on a no-kids boat vacation." Looking down at the floor, not wanting to make eye contact with her concerned grandmother, Julie searched for an excuse to let out her separation anxiety. "And I don't care about this stupid tree either." Julie yanked on one of the fresh branches, pulling the tree over and onto the floor. Grampa, who was lying underneath tightening the stand, got a quick startle. Luckily for Gramma's oversized living room, nothing was broken.

"Up to your room young lady." Grampa, who had remained silent throughout the entire length of Julie's misconduct, was direct and to the point.

Whenever Grampa spoke up, Julie knew that she had gone too far. Turning out of the living room, she began a slow, deliberate climb up the many steps to her third floor attic bedroom.

Halfway up the large front hall staircase, she lingered a moment, noticing all the framed family pictures hanging on the wall. "I wonder if anybody else has as many problems with little brothers as I do," mumbled Julie to herself.

If I could have just held on to it, she thought, *I could have put it in a gumball machine or put it in my blue plastic poodle bank. I could have hid it under my paperweight snow globe of France. Or I could have put it in with my two pet hamsters that Grampa named Dino and Frank.*

At the Needles' farm, Julie had her own bedroom. Joe and Ida Mae's house was so big, they gave each of their grandchildren their own room. At home, which was very nearby, she and Jodi had to share. As Julie wandered through her various collections - posters, toys, and keepsakes - she slowly got ready for bed.

Winter gusts shook the hilltop house. Julie looked out of the third floor window of the converted attic. She could just make out the hemlock grove under the darkening sky. Tiger Lily sat right next to her.

"You know, Tiger Lily, it doesn't matter what I wished for, because the penny in the bottom of the well doesn't have any wishing power. Not yet."

"Meow?"

"That's right. Not until it falls into the water. Those are the rules, and I didn't make 'em up. So I can still wish for any old silly thing, if I want. How would you like to be a cartoon cupid? Or maybe I could wish for something even more silly. How would you like to be a goose?"

"Meow?"

"Julie." Gramma was standing at the door. There was a moment of silence between them, then Gramma sat down on the bed next to her and held her hand. "Honey, I know you miss your mom and dad, and I'm sure they're thinking about you too. Tomorrow, they're going to call around noon. Julie? You know how sometimes you just want to play with your friends your own age, and you don't want Brian or Jodi or your parents… or an' old Gramma lady like me hanging around?"

Julie tried not to smile, but Gramma could always soften her up.

"Well sometimes, parents just want to be with a lot of other people their own age too. In any case, 'The-Clown-Lady-In-The…' what was it?"

"The Clown-Lady-In-The-Circus-Licking-A-Sucker-Wearing-A-Pointy-Witches'-Hat tree."

"No harm done. She's on her feet again."

"It's not a lady, it's just a tree. It was Jodi's stupid idea that all trees were unique and each one had its own special personality. Well I don't believe it."

"But they do, dear," Gramma said, reaching over to scratch Tiger Lily's ears. "Goodnight. Sweet dreams." And with that, Ida Mae was out the door and down the stairs to finish making Christmas, Christmas.

Julie turned off the little lamp next to the bed. She was still not convinced, but Gramma was seldom wrong about such things. Warm and cozy under Gramma's quilt, and with Tiger Lily snuggled up close, Julie's mind continued to wander.

"So… how would you like to be a silver spruce tree with long white whisker needles, Hmm?" And I could be Princess Needles."

"Purr, purr, purr." Tiger Lily dug her way gently into the covers, making the perfect nest in which to sleep.

Dreamy thoughts mixed with the regret she was beginning to feel. "The first thing I'll do tomorrow morning is tell Gramma and Grampa I'm sorry," she whispered to herself. The self-admission of bad behavior released her from the building tension.

"Do you see the people in the trees, Tiger Lily?" she asked. "'Cause I sure don't. I wish we were tree people. Then we might understand what Jodi is talking about." Whispering to herself she said, "If only we could all go back nine days. That's when Mommy and Daddy left. Maybe then the rest of us could go off to some magical new land, too - someplace with all kinds of fantastical new things we've never ever seen before." Julie now imagined herself flying through the air. She was enveloped in a colorful world of Christmas trees and candy and wrapping paper and ribbons, and all the wonderful things that Gramma had created in order to ease her apprehensions. Finally, drifting off in a warm winter's slumber, Julie envisioned dancing gingerbread men, and trees with personalities.

Outside, the storm, which had been slowly inching its way towards the farm, was up to full speed. Whipping winds stirred up a whiteout of blinding snow. Shaking and knocking against each other, the age-old hemlocks swayed in the stormy night. The hard weather would pass, they knew, as it always had during the one hundred or more years that these trees had lived there. They just had to bend a little, and all would be fine.

Suddenly, the force of the wind snapped off a huge limb from one of the towering giants. Down fell the heavy hemlock branch directly onto the roof of the old well. With a thumping thud, one of the icicles dangling from the little roof broke off. Racing faster and faster, the frozen spear fell into the darkness. The ice on which the penny sat broke. And into the deep cold water, Julie's penny sank.

The end of Chapter Three

Chapter Four: Sleepy Twist

A bright white morning beamed through the big country kitchen. Steamy heat from the fresh-baked morning muffins crystallized on the cold window-panes. Mugs of hot cocoa, one for each of her grandchildren, were topped off with whipped cream. While Ida Mae was pleasantly making the morning meal, Julie lay in her snuggly bed, completely covered by her colorful patchwork quilt. Gramma's voice was the perfect wake up.

"Rise and shine. Breakfast is ready… lots to do."

Julie lowered her quilted cover. Glancing around her old-fashioned bed-room, she squinted at the wind up clock on the nightstand. It was 7:45 a.m.

Downstairs, dishes were being placed upon the big table, along with nap-kins and juice glasses. Julie could hear her Gramma's voice calling to her again. "I have fresh-baked orange-peel corn muffins… your favorite."

"Aaaah." A big yawning stretch, and Julie stood up. Tiger Lily had already opened the door to go out. Taking her first wobbly, just-out-of-bed Christmas morning steps, she stopped to look at herself in the full-length mirror on the back of the bedroom door.

"Eeek!" She screamed a quick shocking peep of a scream that ended in a breathless gasp and a long, silent stare.

Who is that? What is that? she thought. That couldn't be me. Am I green? I am green! It was true. Pine needles were glued to her face, stuck to her hair, and layered on her arms. If this was a dream, she should only have to speak aloud to convince herself it was only a dream, and bring herself fully awake. Still, the tree-girl stared out at her from the looking glass.

Seeking answers, she ran out of her room and barged into Jodi's. Lying there on top of the covers reading a book, Jodi had been altered as well. She, too, had been turned into a tree. A tree that could talk, a tree with two arms, two hands, and two feet. How was this possible?

"You're a tree! I'm a tree!"

Jodi looked up. "Yeah, so what's your point?"

Puzzled by her younger sister's sudden peculiar comments, Jodi replied, "And so is Gramma and Grampa, Mom, Dad. But I think Uncle Peter is a modified shrub."

"How did we get here?" stammered Julie.

"Is this a bees-and-pollen question? Because if so, ask Gramma. I'm not in the mood."

Jodi threw herself back on the big pillow headboard and continued to read. The book she was focused on was entitled, "Seedling Psychology."

Realizing that this situation might have something to do with the magic penny, Julie blurted out what was on her mind. "This is all Brian's fault!"

Jodi looked up from her reading material. "My diagnosis is that you are suffering from middle seedling syndrome, and, as a result, imagined post-nursery episodes are once again flaring up. Treatment? I suggest you pinch yourself."

Easy for her to say, thought Julie. *Pinch myself? Where would I start? At my needled tip-top or around the bottom of my branches?* Besides, it was hard for Julie to take anything Jodi said seriously because... well... she was a tree. After all, just hours ago Julie had gotten her real human sister really annoyed.

Fun and scary, scary and fun, these two very opposite emotions were bubbling over inside Julie. Like the scary fun that she felt just before the jerking and bumping little red car, pushed into the mysterious doorway of the 'Laugh in the Dark' funhouse last summer. The only difference now was that she wasn't wrapped in her father's big arms. And she didn't have her mother's hand to hold on to.

Walking into the upstairs hall, trying to believe that she was real, Julie stopped to inspect how it was that she could move. Looking down she saw that she had on her pink rubber boots. She wiggled her toes inside. They moved. Then slowly she lifted her right foot out to see what it had become. Her lower shin was covered with bark. Below was a hard, knotted ankle, and farther down, a bare exposed heel. Her foot had become a huge root. She had no real toes, but five wriggly smaller roots that moved just like toes. To the sides of her feet and all along the bottom, clusters of little roots softened her every step. When she put her foot back into the boot, she discovered that the boot was filled with moist muddy muck.

Her hands, covered by Goodwill mittens, moved just like her old hands. Slowly she removed one of the mittens. There was a wrist, covered with tree bark, and the back of her hand was covered in bark as well. Turning her hand over, she saw that the bark faded on her palm. It was smooth and grainy. Her fingers were all bright green. The sprouts were the kind that she had seen on the sides of trees in late spring that hadn't yet been pruned. This was a lot to comprehend. Standing at the top of the staircase, she quickly put her mitten back on. While contemplating her next move, she was greeted by Tiger Lily.

"Purr, purr, purr." The happy cat said hello to Julie as always, by buzzing around her feet.

"Oh no, not you too Tiger Lily!" Her healthy, jolly, best friend of a cat had also been transformed into a green creature. Tiger Lily resembled a mini pine tree that had somehow grown sideways. The tip of her nose was pointed. She got wider at her mouth and eyes, and her ears protruded just a little beyond her thick, bushy shape. The fat, happy farm cat's whiskers were yellowish green, and a pattern of green tiger-stripes encircled her all the way back to the widest part of her body. Her raccoonish tail lifted high, as always, but now it too was green. Circular stripes of light, dark, light, dark, and lighter and darker than green - almost black green - patterned her pine bough of a tail all the way to the needled tip-top. Four little legs, covered in silky balsa needle green fur, were accented with brown pinecone paws.

Clank, clank, clank, clank! Clank, clank, clank, clank!

The sound of a clanking dish in the kitchen was heard. In an instant, Tiger Lily raced down the stairs to see what there was to eat. It appeared that even though everyone had become some kind of tree, some things still remained the same.

As Julie descended the stairs, all the images of her relatives had also changed. Uncle Lenny, no longer tall, lean and blonde, was also green, as was her cousin Natalie. And her great aunt Helen, Ida Mae's sister, posed with a large tree grin. "They've all been changed into trees, just like me," she said aloud.

Whoosh! Sliding down the banister past her was Brian. He too was transformed.

I must be sleep-dream-walking, she thought to herself. Stepping slowly through the family farmhouse, everything was as it was when she went to bed, yet somehow different. It was brighter and more colorful than yesterday. The chairs, the floors… even the doorknobs. She glanced into the living room where Grampa had set up the holiday tree the night before. It was gone. There weren't any decorations, either. All the booties, cards, and handmade collectibles that had been there the night before were no longer. Was this a joke? A punishment? Ida Mae could be heard humming. In complete bewilderment, Julie walked toward the pleasant sounds emanating from the kitchen.

"Gramma?" Julie stood face-to-face with her beloved, newly green Nana.

"Yes dear?" Not thinking anything was wrong, Ida Mae continued the kitchen chores.

Ida Mae no longer had her curly brown hair with the little gray here and there that Julie remembered. But the eyeglasses she wore were still the same, and so was the apron she had tied to her front. And so, too, the warmth in her eyes that Julie loved most still remained.

Julie decided to speak. "What happened to Christmas?"

"What do you mean Honey? Nothing happened to it. It's still on the calendar." Ida Mae pointed to the big calendar on the back of the door, "And only nine days away! See?" This reality was now even more bizarre. Not only had she and her family been turned into trees, but it was now only the sixteenth, nine days prior to a Christmas that still hadn't arrived.

Brian came up from under the breakfast table to sit across from Julie. He paid no attention to Julie, and concentrated on his big plate of food. His bark covered lips gobbled like an eating machine.

Ida Mae put a big muffin on the plate in front of Julie. "Eat your muffin, Sweetie." Then she bent down to give Tiger Lily a bowl of milk. The happy cat purred and lapped up her breakfast with a sap-colored tongue.

"I need to talk to Grampa. It's really important." Julie took a nibble of her muffin.

"Brian, quick, take the rest of these baked goods to your grampa." Brian ran off with a basket of goodies laughing. "The big storm last night practically covered your Great Aunt Sylvia's house with snow. Your grampa is going to help dig her out. Candyville was hit pretty hard."

"Candyville?" asked Julie.

"You know, the little village just past the big rock candy quarry. We went there for a family picnic some years back."

Julie didn't remember any picnic, or Candyville for that matter. "How long will he be gone? I really need to ask him something!"

"Oh, a couple of days. It'll be just us girls and Brian until he gets back. What's the problem? Maybe I can help you."

Julie took another bite of her muffin and a sip of hot cocoa. "Do you know anything about magic? Because I need to find some. Quick. But I can't tell you why."

Ida Mae sat next to Julie, eating her scrambled eggs and toast. "The only magic I know of that doesn't require a birthday or losing a tooth would be the Gingertown Christmas Eve Pageant."

Ida Mae pulled Julie's face close to her own, to inspect her mouth. "Say ahh..."

"Ahh."

"No." Ida Mae had eliminated one possible reason for Julie's question. "Whoever wins the pageant gets loads of super gifts and ten minutes worth of magic crown wishes starting at midnight, Christmas Eve."

That was it, as far as Julie was concerned. Here was the answer to her current dilemma. "I'll do it. I know I can win!"

Standing up to pour herself some juice, Ida Mae didn't want to burst the child's bubble, but she had to stop the excited nine year old. "No, no, no, Honey. You're too young to enter."

"Too young?" Thinking on her feet, as always, Julie quickly had a new plan. "How 'bout you Gramma? Look how pretty you are."

As far as trees were concerned, Julie thought her Gramma Needles was stunning. She had a full bushy shape that didn't need to be pruned. Her color was deep and, if she were only covered in tinsel, Gramma would be the grandest tree of all.

Flattered, almost blushing, Ida Mae responded. "Thank you, dear, but I believe that all the participants must be between 16 and 26 years of age."

Slumping down in her chair Julie resumed her breakfast. Jodi, who had just finished a chapter in her book, stood in the doorway to the kitchen. The once tall skinny girl with long hippie hair and studious reading glasses was now a tall, gappy, skinny tree with studious reading glasses. Not full or plump with branches like her grandmother, Jodi took after the more natural trees that Julie remembered from her walks through the farm. These were the trees that never got pruned. They always appealed to those customers in search of an old-fashioned, sparse Christmas tree look.

While examining her sister, Julie's eyes got wider. Somehow, Tiger Lily knew what the little planner was thinking and commented.

"Meow?"

Julie sprung to her feet. "Good morning, big sister dear!"

"Are you sick?"

As Julie swiftly guided Jodi to her place at the table, Jodi felt like she was being pushed through the line in the cafeteria at school. *Kerplop!* Julie pushed Jodi down into the chair. In puzzled silence, Jodi and Ida Mae watched as a scurry of muffins, eggs, toast, fruit, juice, and hot cocoa appeared in front of Jodi. Before Jodi could put the muffin in her mouth, Julie shouted, "No, not yet!" Stopping in mid-bite, Jodi held the orange-peel and corn treat still. Julie frantically rummaged through the kitchen junk drawer. She found what she was looking for. Slapping the muffin out of Jodi's hand and back onto the plate, Julie jammed a fist full of little candles into it and lit them.

"I forgot to congratulate you, big sister. You just had your birthday. Silly me!"

"Yeah. In September. Are you still in tiny tree dementia land?"

Phew! Brian popped up unexpectedly to blow out the candles. Ida Mae took the muffin away.

"I hear that Gingertown gives brand new cars to 16-year-old beauty queens."

Julie's intentions were now becoming apparent. Jodi was not amused. "I would rather be strapped face down to a buzz saw in a toothpick factory than do that mindless, 'Look at me! I'm pretty with no brains' contest."

Not willing to give up, Julie just had to find a way. "Think of all the prizes."

"And what do you get?" Jodi figured there had to be an angle to Julie's request.

"The crown."

"Aha! I thought so. I thought so!" Jodi was well aware of her little sister's material obsessions.

"I need it. It has magic powers."

"Magic? Don't be ridiculous!" Jodi, always a firm believer in the practical, the provable, the "give me evidence" aspects of life, found Julie's answer both laughable and sad. "That is just more commercial hype designed to manipulate pathetic little Christmas tree wannabes suffering from delusions of grandeur."

Ida Mae was not pleased by Jodi's assessment. "Does that make me a former wannabe? I was a contestant once, you know."

"Women didn't know they were being exploited when you were a girl Gramma. But now that we do know, it's time for change."

Sitting quietly for a moment Julie decided to take a new approach. With dramatic flair, she stood up on the chair and began preaching to both sister and Grandmother. "I am appalled at this treatment of young trees. You should all be covered in gypsy moths and Japanese beetles for what you've done here today." Any local politician would have been proud of the way she delivered her address.

Julie jumped off the chair just as abruptly, and once again began rummaging through the kitchen junk drawer.

"*Now* what are you doing?" Jodi was as surprised as ever. This was a new high for her already over-dramatic little sister.

Julie returned to the table with a pen and a pad. "I'm writing your acceptance speech. After your historic victory, a declaration of your principles must be heard." Holding her pen up to her lips, Julie pretended it was a microphone. "Now tell us Miss Needles, or is it Noodles? As the winner of the annual Gingertown Pageant, do you have any words for our readers?"

Playing along, Jodi responded with psychoanalytical flair. "The other contestants are suffering from borderline personality disorder, and with a marked propensity toward mood swings ranging from extreme and overt narcissism to multiple personality disorder."

Julie made a stern reporter face. "Could you say that in plain English?"

"Certainly! They're all nasty, backstabbing, stuck-up, and two-faced. Simply put, they're all pathetic!"

Unable to contain their laughter the two girls and their grandmother shared a hilarious moment.

Beauty. Pageant. Debutante. Beauty. Pageant. Debutante. No matter how many times Jodi repeated those three little words in her mind, all she could think of was *Fake. Plastic. Empty.* "Have you ever tried to have a conversation with girls that think they're pretty?" she contemplated aloud. "Oh how I wish I could 'zing-zab' everyone of them."

"What would you do?" Julie was eager to hear how her sister would handle such a situation.

"I have this secret fantasy." A nerve had been struck. Jodi vented to Julie and Ida Mae as never before.

"While sitting in study hall watching them apply eye shadow, I use my telekinetic powers to lock us all in. Click, click, snap, klack, click. They all stop for a lip-gloss second, their mouths frozen open as they look up from their hand-held mini-makeup-mirrors. A silent wide-eyed fear leaches through the conceited after-school Cosmetic Club crowd. It is then that they realize, like flies trapped in a mayonnaise jar, that no matter how hard they buzz against the glass, there is no escape. They run screaming. I look. I point. I freeze them in their roots. Not one of them can move. They shiver as I pull out a portable insecticide spray pump from under my coat. I give the ominous canister a quick compression pump. *Ka-chunk, Ka-chunk, Ka-chunk.* They beg me, 'Please, Jodi, Noooo! Don't expose our less than ordinary complexions.' I approach slowly as they all shake with fright. Then the horror of all horrors: I blast liquid 'Fungi Be Gone' on all of them."

"What happens next?" Even Gramma wanted to hear the end of this tale.

"Layers and layers of painted gunk drips off all of their faces. Makeup slides off cheeks and chins, melting away their high-and-mighty cosmetic attitudes. Then, before I will allow a single debutante-wannabe to leave, I dunk their empty, treetop heads in buckets of cold water. And then I make them all write 5000 times..."

"5000 times?" Julie was impressed.

"Yes, 5000 times… in a notebook: 'I will not allow myself to be brain-washed by television and magazines!'"

Gramma was speechless for a moment. "I hope I never get on your bad side." She chuckled and went back to cleaning up the kitchen.

"Beauty comes from within," declared Jodi. "All their vapid little brains can do is shop." Standing up to imitate them she spoke in a high-pitched voice. "'Vapid? What does that mean? Is it a salad dressing?'"

Julie jumped in, "You mean the girls that stand around at the food court, right?"

"Exactly. 'I have no brain. I don't do math, and please don't ask me to spell it.'"

Julie playing along with Jodi adding, "Should we sound out the word first? 'Va-pid.'"

Both girls giggled and agreed for once. "They are all pathetic!"

Jodi had convinced herself, with Julie's help, that it was time to take a stand. "I will enter the pageant. It's time to teach those woodpecker beauty-brains a lesson."

United in a common goal, the two sisters went back upstairs to plan for the contest. Ida Mae was proud that her two granddaughters were finally working together.

A few minutes later, the phone rang.

"Hello?"

It was Redda Pinesky. Redda was a one-woman information bank. If any gossip needed to be heard, she heard it. And if any bit of information needed to be shared, she shared and shared and shared. "Ida darling… how are you? It's Redda, your over-the-hilltop-and-down-the-road neighbor."

"How are you today, Redda? Yes the storm was a doozey! And yes, Joe is on his way to Sylvia's as we speak."

Redda's low, groveling voice filled Ida Mae's ear. "I either had to call you or bust a pinecone. This year the pageant will be televised."

51

Ida Mae was shocked. This was news, real news and not just gossip. Redda continued, "And your wonderful, tall, very natural-looking Jodi will be entering the contest? Hmm?"

"My, my, news travels fast."

As always, Redda was on top of everything. Jodi had called Margaret, who called Hannah, who told her mother Zelda, who called Gracie, who called Redda.

"Congratulations Ida, on not giving up on the family-tree dream. Too bad not all of us can be pageant winners."

Redda used every opportunity to remind all who had competed over the years, and lost, that she had been victorious. Not ever wanting to give Redda the satisfaction of seeing how this got her goat, Ida Mae feigned indifference by always quoting the wrong year.

"Yes. You did it in '59. "

"'61," Redda corrected. "But who remembers that I did it in a red garland with silver glitter stars evening gown? Wasn't I gorgeous?"

Reluctantly, but as a habit of conversation, Ida Mae agreed with Redda. "Gorgeous."

"And can you believe it? I have even more wonderful news! My sweet sixteen-year-old granddaughter will be entering the pageant too. It will be just like old times. My La Cona will wear the crown! And your Jodi can hold her cape while she poses for photographers. Gotta go now."

Click. Redda had hung up.

That Redda! thought Ida Mae. *Somebody oughta spray her with Fungi Be Gone.*

The end of Chapter Four

Chapter Five: Problem Solving

Lying on her bed, Jodi was talking up a storm on her cell phone. "I can see it now, me telling everybody how stupid this is." Jodi had clearly committed herself to yet another brand-new cause. She was going to teach the world a lesson about inner beauty.

Ida Mae, overhearing Jodi's last comments, looked into Jodi's room. "A word of advice: If you want to win, I suggest you stop telling your leaf-mealy-mouthed friends how stupid the contest is." Jodi hung up quickly.

From out in the hall, Gramma dragged a big box into Jodi's bedroom. The conversation with Redda spurred Ida Mae. "How dare Redda assume that just because she had won her granddaughter will too!" she mumbled to herself as she dragged a big box into Jodi's room. "Jodi has just as much of a chance as any other contestant."

Smiling at her granddaughters, Ida Mae said, "I never knew why I held on to these for so many years. It might have been because in the back of my mind, I always thought that one day I'd be able to pass them on, and today is that day."

"Surprise!" Brian sprang out of the box of old collectibles. Somehow he had managed to sneak inside it when no one was looking. Then, as Gramma helped Brian untangle himself, she showed the girls the contents of the box. "These were my old pageant decorations."

Julie and Jodi had never seen any of these before. The two curious girls each put on a pair of glass Christmas ball earrings and swung their heads back and forth to make the balls swing.

"They're old-fashioned pretty, but with some jazzy modifications they might do just fine. As you girls have often reminded me, we live in a modern, televised world."

Jodi and Julie blurted it out in perfect unison. "We heard the news, too!"

"This being the first televised pageant, the competition will be fierce." Gramma warned.

Julie, loving a good challenge, was excited by this. "Fierce sounds fun!"

"I made a list." Gramma pulled it from her apron pocket, gazed down at it, and then spoke. "Jodi, first stand up and take off your slippers. Now I want you to put these athletic flats on."

Jodi did as requested. "They feel a little big." They looked more like over-sized clown shoes.

"Now stand still. Julie, help me put these on your sister."

From within a very old box, Gramma uncovered a collection of vintage teacups. Quickly, she began to hang them from as many of Jodi's limb tips as possible. Julie helped. There were blue china types, rose floral patterns, as well as gold and silver rimmed hand-painted little cups. Some of the cups had chips, and others were perfect porcelain specimens. Dainty sized miniatures to manly-sized mugs.

Then Ida Mae handed Julie a basket full of various lengths of cotton laun-dry rope. "Drape these from the top of Jodi's head to the bottom of her bushy skirt," said Gramma. Together they emptied the basket of cut rope onto the potential new beauty queen. When the decorations were all on, crazy as these items were, a unique, antique, original style emerged that was hard to describe.

"You want me to wear teacups, tennis shoes and laundry line to the pageant?" Jodi was at a loss.

"No… and, well, yes. The teacups will strengthen your limbs, and teach you poise and balance. The laundry line will force you to move with ladylike dignity - whether sitting, standing, or gracefully passing through any room. If you plop yourself down on the sofa like a sack of fertilizer, then you will get all tangled up in a big knot. The oversized athletic shoes will force you to be aware of every step you take. If you move too fast, you'll trip. If you run up the stairs, you will trip. If you take monster steps without thinking, you will trip. None of these are the real fashion trims. These are all just practice pieces."

Ida Mae looked once again at her paper note. "If you can't walk and chew gum at the same time without falling flat on your face, then you will never become a champion. And, while you are practicing walking around your room, up and down the front stairs and around the living room, I want you to repeat a simple vocal exercise. It goes like this…

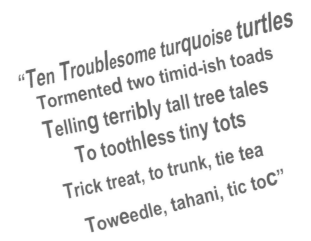

"Ten Troublesome turquoise turtles
Tormented two timid-ish toads
Telling terribly tall tree tales
To toothless tiny tots
Trick treat, to trunk, tie tea
Toweedle, tahani, tic toc"

Before Jodi could concentrate on a single syllable of Gramma's tongue twister, first she had to try to make at least one small circle around her room. "I had no idea how hard all this could be." Slowly, slowly she managed to complete her circle. Her grandmother fed her the words to repeat aloud as she circled the room once more. "Ten… troublesome turquoise turtles… tormented..." It was working! Ida Mae's method of building runway confidence was taking root.

"I had completely forgotten about this tongue twister, until my conversation with Redda." Ida Mae was beaming.

"Augh!" *Crash!* Tiger Lily jumped straight up in the air. Jodi collapsed.

Brian poked his head out of the closet giggling.

"Not to worry," Gramma reassured Jodi. "Practice, practice, practice and you will learn to become a solid opponent. Julie, I want you to go into town. Take your brother with you." Ida Mae handed another list to Julie.

"Alone with Brian? But he… How?" Julie was mortified. Brian stuck his head out from under the bed, this time flaunting his green tongue at her.

"Yes alone with Brian. It's time the two of you learned to get along. You're a big girl now. I know you can do it."

In a whispery, snotty, mimicking voice Brian continued to taunt Julie while crawling under the bed. "Yes, you're a big, big, super monster fat girl now. It's time you stop being a booger head."

"But." Julie made a deflated face of defeat because she knew her grandmother was right.

"Your grampa is digging out Great Aunt Sylvia and I have to go see Mrs. Juniper."

Gramma rushed to put on her winter hat, gloves, and coat. The two children fol-lowed, also getting bundled up for the outside.

"Just follow the instructions on the note sweetie!" Ida Mae shouted with glee, and hurried up over the hilltop through the fresh fallen snow.

Rolling white hills covered with fresh deep-freeze stretched as far as tree-eyes could see. What used to be cultivated rows of scotch pines were now rows of oversized candy sculptures. Lollipop sticks the size of lampposts were covered with gobs of jellybean-shaped buds.

A "waste no time" project was at hand, but Julie just had to stop for a few moments to see how her world had changed. If all the plants look like candy trees, she thought, then maybe the snow wasn't actually snow. Perhaps it was sugar covered frosting! She stood next to one of the many towering candy creations that were scattered throughout the newly envisioned Needles' Farm. Taking caution, she opened her mouth to taste the snow.

"Hmm. It's cold like snow. It melts like snow. But it's just the slightest bit sweet. Mmm!"

Without warning, the branch she had just tasted surprisingly shook. All the snow, which was just overhead, fell on her head in one clean thump.

Who else but Brian. One quick shimmy-shake, and off it all fell. Being a tree was similar to being a duck, she thought. The many needles that covered her fluffed up like feathers.

"We have to go. Now!" Brian demanded. "Gramma says you gotta take me."

Julie and Brian made their way down the snowy path to the main road, then up the hill towards the public transportation stop. The lush forest growth Julie remembered had all turned into colorful candy-scapes. All this was more than Julie could ever have dreamed of.

As she strolled with eyes aglow, she couldn't help but smile at the world she miss-wished upon herself, even though Julie knew she was in a real pickle of a dilemma. *The pageant's a good thing for everybody,* thought Julie. Jodi had her new teenage cause, Gramma was happily reliving a memory, Brian had a whole new pile of trouble he could get into, and she herself might somehow find the magic she needed to return to the world she once knew.

The small freestanding little windbreak stood where it always had. It was a weathered, red, three-sided structure open in the front. The back wall had a small four-pane window. Julie remembered how she helped her Grampa fix the glass last summer. It was fun, and she was glad the little shack was still here.

"Hello Julie. And this is little Brian." It was Redda Pinesky. Even though she was now a tree, her voice and personality were unmistakable. Surprisingly, Mrs. Pinesky's plump figure was more beautiful than ever. Julie began to see the former world she once knew in a brighter light. As trees, beauty somehow had a completely different set of standards.

Redda had become what Grampa would call, "the overly-pruned variety." The overly-pruned types were clipped and clipped and clipped into a geometric cone shape that was completely unnatural. "City folk want it to look more artificial, but still be real," he would explain every spring, as he and his crew reshaped the fresh growth. It made no sense to Grampa Joe, but still, they were mighty popular. Redda was definitely overly pruned. Covering her perfect cone of a physique, she had on a knitted afghan with an attached hood.

"Where's your grandmother Ida?" inquired Redda.

"Visiting Mrs. Juniper."

Redda's eyes opened wider, as always happened when her detective-type personality became pleased with itself. "Borrowing the sewing machine I bet. Oh, some things never change." Feeling pleased with her deductions, Redda continued. "Have you met my granddaughter, La Cona, and her new friend, Cypress Limb?"

Standing just behind Redda towards the back of the slant roof protection stood two slimmer trees. The two of them were covered completely from the top to the bottom with layers of fashionable fabrics. Their coverings resembled fancy hoop skirts, the kind that Julie remembered seeing at her cousin's wedding. The only little bit of tree she could see were two green faces. They even had on scarves and hats under their hooded cloaks.

La Cona spoke first, with just the slightest southern inflection. "I'm visiting from South Carolina."

Cypress Limb's dialect was one that Julie had never heard before. "And I'm visiting from Kentucky. Ooo, it's so cold here, how do you stand it?"

La Cona, huddling as far in the corner of the little shed as possible, shivering as she spoke. "Our delicate needles haven't grown accustomed to the northern winds yet."

"Aren't they lovely?" Redda bragged. "Needles as soft as silk. And look at those figures! Just like me back when I was a pageant winner. I wore a red garland dress with silver stars… in '61. Tell your sister Jodi I wish her luck and hope to heaven she doesn't get needle-fright like her grandmother did."

Gramma had certainly never mentioned any of this before. And what on earth was "needle-fright?"

La Cona and Cypress shared a sarcastic snicker with one another. Recoiling a bit, Redda was pleased. She had disclosed information that just might help undermine the competition. The odd part of Redda's ever-adolescent maneuverings was that she had no adult regard for the ears she spilled her gossip upon, even when those ears belonged to a child.

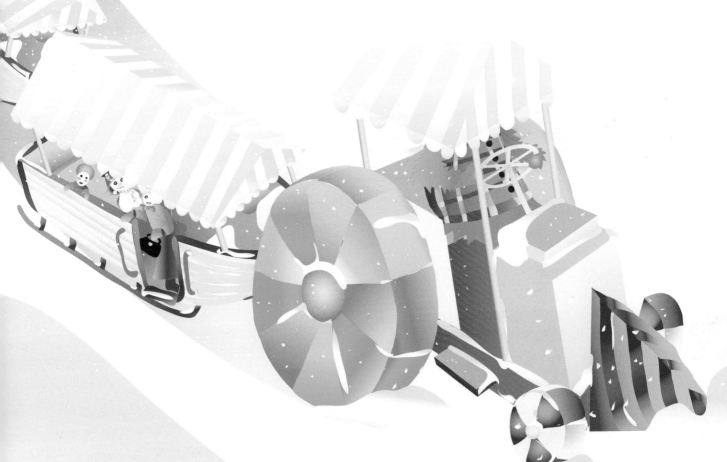

"Oh, maybe I shouldn't have mentioned it. Some family secrets are best kept from the little ones."

Although Julie was only nine, she too knew how to milk information out of a conversation. Pretending to know all the facts she responded with a positive poker face, "Of course Gramma told us. We all had a big laugh."

Not paying attention to the conversation, Brian was busy licking the sled stop sign pole. It was made of red and white striped peppermint. Noticing Brian's current fascination, Redda spoke softy and directly to Julie. "When the judges asked poor Ida the final question, her needles just started dropping off."

Redda bent down even closer to Julie's ear. "It was the talk of the pageant. 'Needle-less' to say, I was crowned Pageant Queen. I hear it's passed down on the mother's side, but with all the new-fangled cosmetics, it shouldn't be a problem. Tell your sister to soak herself in a sap oil bath for twenty minutes every night before she goes to bed. Then to wrap herself in…" Redda's advice was cut short by the approaching sled bus. Merry-go-round bells could be heard.

The front of the moving vehicle was a snow tractor with massive wheels. Brian jumped up and down with glee upon seeing it. High above the engine sat the driver in a small-enclosed cab, where he navigated the road holding on to a big yellow steering wheel.

"I'm going to be a sled bus driver when I grow up!" exclaimed Brian.

Behind the sputtering tractor, two oversized passenger rowboats with railed bottoms glided along the frozen highway. Each was an open-air rider with yellow-and-white striped canvas awnings overhead. Connecting hitches linked the two carriers like train cars. A "V" shaped plow, mounted on the front, sprayed snow onto the little sled shack as it slid to a halt.

Redda, La Cona and Cypress were covered with fresh white snow. They quickly shook it off with distaste. Julie and Brian giggled.

"Hello, ladies," announced the driver from way atop his driver's cab. Brian popped up from behind the group. The driver, seeing Brian, continued, "And little seedling too. You are all looking especially green this frosty morning. A very busy day today."

"Douglas, how are you? And how is your wife Donna?" Redda knew everybody.

Doug the sled bus driver was a long-needled fir tree. Positioned just under his very green nose was a super bushy silvery-green moustache. His eyebrows were the same color and a spray of silver needles also poked out of the tall plaid hat he wore. "Donna and the saplings are all charged up, with the TV folk coming into to town. It's all the buzz."

Redda agreed, "It is exciting."

Julie helped Brian into the passenger boat. The riders already on board were a variety of creatures. Each nodded "hello" to Julie as she and Brian got seats.

There were talking snow people, crying gumdrop babies being held by lollipop parents, whispering chocolate ladies, and gingerbread cookie men. All were consumed with one topic of conversation: a coast-to-coast broadcast from their own little town.

"Christmas will never be the same, now that Gingertown will be seen on television."

"Imagine all the tourists! We'll make gobs of money."

"Just think! We'll be in all the papers. Maybe I can turn my house into a bed and breakfast."

The excited conversations faded from Julie's attention as the sled bus slid along the winding country road. Situated at the bottom of the valley, surrounded by picturesque hills, there it was. Gingertown. It was just like Gramma's gingerbread village in the bakeshop, but bigger. Much bigger. A variety of practical but highly decorative structures were all clustered together in a quaint fairytale way. Julie gazed upon the oversized dark molasses gingerbread houses, steep-gabled medium tan sugar cookie shops and a bank made of sliced fruitcake. Pastel pink iced sugar cookie columns lined the front of the Post Office and log-sized pretzel street posts held candy signs with licorice-whip scripted letters on them. Chocolate chip cookie sled bus stop benches stood at every corner.

Colorful patterns of frosting, mosaics made from miniature cinnamon hearts, and a host of other wonderful, beautiful, edible details filled Julie's senses. Sweet snow-covered wonders were at every turn.

"Last stop!" driver Doug shouted in his very comical manner. "Everybody out. And please! No licking your names into the seats!" Brian was given a stern look from Doug. Julie and Brian were the last to exit. As the sled bus pulled away, Julie simply stood there in amazement, holding her brother's hand.

The end of Chapter Five

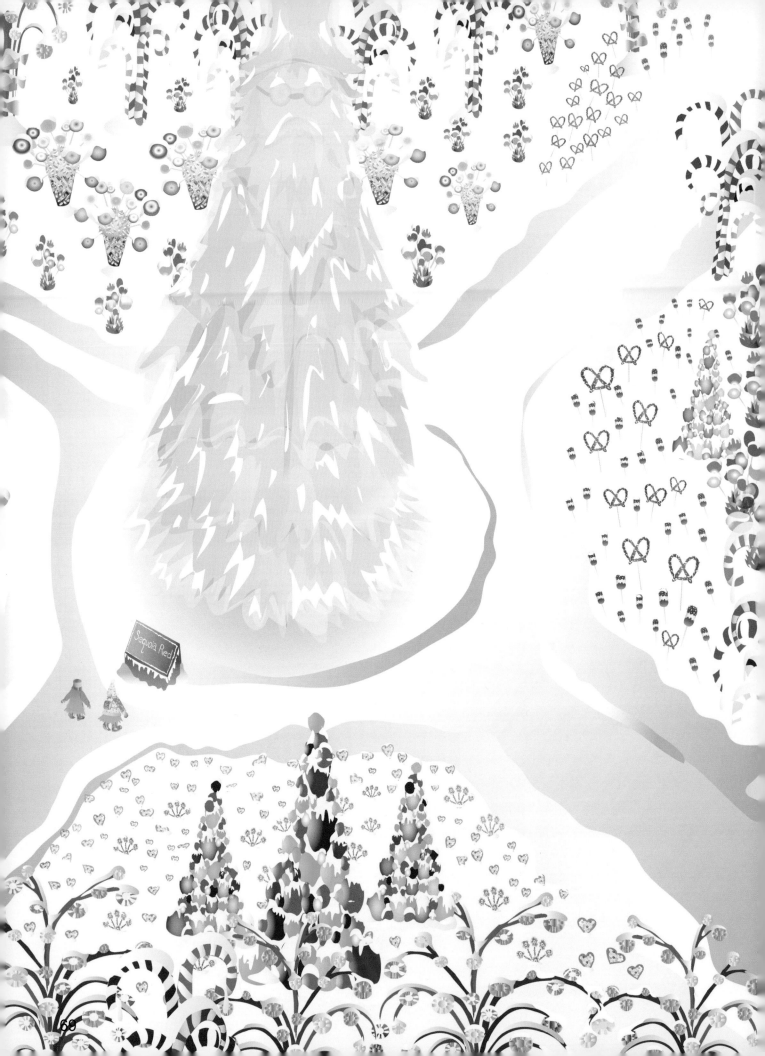

Sequoia Red!

Chapter Six: Gingertown

Taking a deep breath, Julie pulled out the note that Gramma had given her. This was the first time she had gone shopping all on her own. And the first time that she had been anywhere with Brian alone. Gramma wrote,

Number one... Find the pageant office.

"Hmm." Julie inspected the little square that she and Brian were standing in. "There it is." Across the town square was a clearly printed sign:

PAGEANT OFFICE

Julie and Brian made their way through the pretty park. In the middle of it was a glorious fountain. "Wow." They stopped. Both children were speechless. At the back of a frozen reflective pool, an enormous sculpture stood covered in layers and layers of ice. It was the tallest anything in Gingertown. It was taller than the town hall. It was taller than the chocolate lookout tower which stood above the Gingertown Fire Department. It was even taller than the red and white striped spire on the top of the House of Ginger Candy Factory. Julie read the plaque: "This fountain was erected in honor of our beloved founder, Sequoia Red."

"Someday I'm going to be as big as him," declared Brian.

"Someday…" Julie smiled.

The two children proceeded through the town square towards the pageant office and went inside.

Standing face to face with the two little adventurers was Ms. Canadia Hemlock. She spoke in a singsong pattern, which was full of positive pageant energy. "Can I be of assistance?"

"I am here to register my big sister for the Gingertown Christmas Eve Pageant," answered Julie with a big smile.

"Why is your sister not here in person?" The pageant co-coordinator was always direct and to the point.

"She's at home balancing dumb teacups," Brian answered, mimicking the Pageant Lady's sing-songy, almost operatic style of speaking.

Noting Brian's sarcasm, Canadia flashed him a look, which caused Brian's arrogant posture to melt a bit. But then she continued cheerily, passing it off as typical childish behavior. "Teacups? Oh, my life is now complete. How it pleases me to know that all of my hard work has not been in vain." The teacup teaching method had been invented by Canadia. Ms. Hemlock was so taken with the news that the teacup balancing and strengthening method was still being used, it sent a fresh wave of giggling girlish enthusiasm through her.

For as long as anyone could remember Ms. Canadia Hemlock had been known as the Pageant Lady. Her age was anybody's guess. But in her youth, she had written the book, *Standard Pageant Rules, Etiquette, Tips, Tricks and Secrets for Winning.* Proudly, she recited the all "t"s tongue twister.

"Ten troublesome turquoise turtles
Tormented two timid-ish toads

Telling terribly tall tales
To toothless tiny tots

Trick treat, ta trunk, tie tea
Toweedle, tahani, tic tic."

Taking a deep breath and letting out a sigh of contented joy, Canadia was transported to a happier time. She bent down to flit her eyelashes. Up close Julie could smell the aroma of extremely sweet perfume. It was the kind that made her eyes water whenever the counter ladies at the mall gave away sprits samples.

"My experience and pageant wisdom did not come easily. I participated in hundreds of tiny tree tot pageants. Perhaps you might like to enter the challenging world of pageant competition?"

Julie was pleased to be asked. "Do you think I'm pretty enough?"

"Heavens NO! No one is EVER pretty enough! To win you must be as sharp as a rosebush thorn and tougher than a watermelon skin. My mother, bless her bark, saw my potential at a very young age and made me do it."

"Did you ever win any?" Julie asked innocently.

After a gasp of shock, Ms. Hemlock stood proud and perfectly postured. "Did I win? Do these look like the trophies of a loser?" A grand rope with gold tassels was pulled. Slowly, from behind a red velvet curtain, a king's treasure of trophies was revealed.

"Little Miss Sugar Sapper, Tiny Green Queen, Miss Greenhouse Hopeful, Miss Amazing Arbor Club; I won them all."

There were so many prizes that Julie couldn't count them all. Golden, silver-hued, metallic copper, red-trimmed, rhinestone-covered, - every possible combination of honor was on display.

"You won all of these?" Even Brian was impressed.

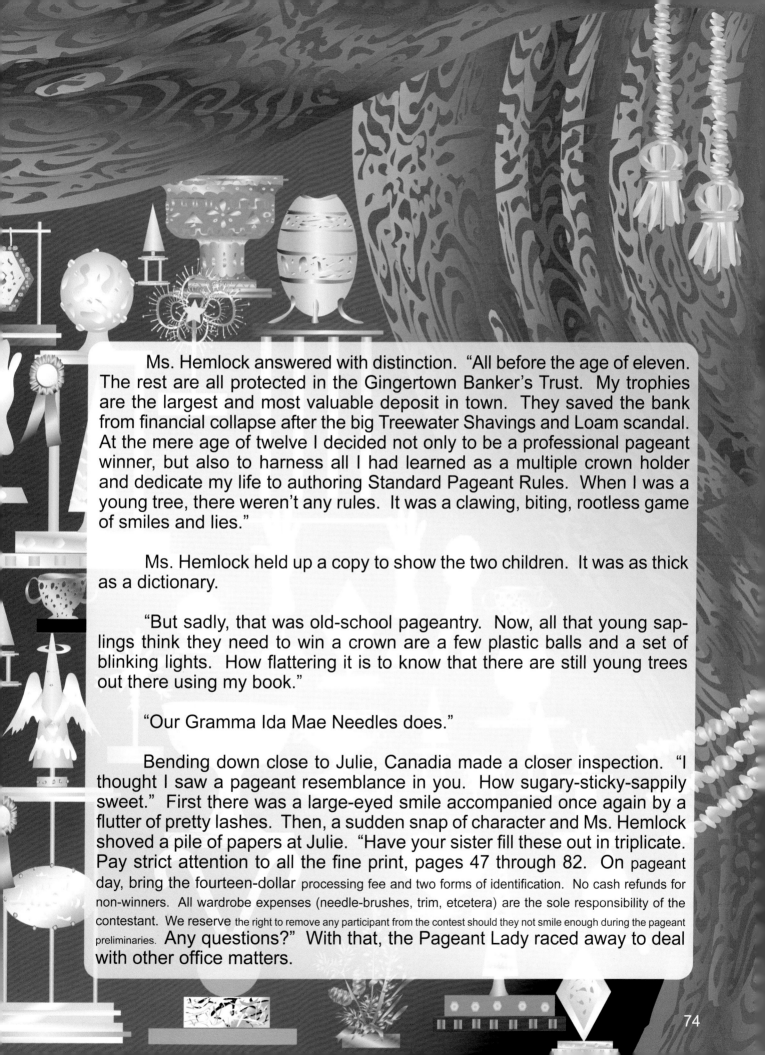

Ms. Hemlock answered with distinction. "All before the age of eleven. The rest are all protected in the Gingertown Banker's Trust. My trophies are the largest and most valuable deposit in town. They saved the bank from financial collapse after the big Treewater Shavings and Loam scandal. At the mere age of twelve I decided not only to be a professional pageant winner, but also to harness all I had learned as a multiple crown holder and dedicate my life to authoring Standard Pageant Rules. When I was a young tree, there weren't any rules. It was a clawing, biting, rootless game of smiles and lies."

Ms. Hemlock held up a copy to show the two children. It was as thick as a dictionary.

"But sadly, that was old-school pageantry. Now, all that young saplings think they need to win a crown are a few plastic balls and a set of blinking lights. How flattering it is to know that there are still young trees out there using my book."

"Our Gramma Ida Mae Needles does."

Bending down close to Julie, Canadia made a closer inspection. "I thought I saw a pageant resemblance in you. How sugary-sticky-sappily sweet." First there was a large-eyed smile accompanied once again by a flutter of pretty lashes. Then, a sudden snap of character and Ms. Hemlock shoved a pile of papers at Julie. "Have your sister fill these out in triplicate. Pay strict attention to all the fine print, pages 47 through 82. On pageant day, bring the fourteen-dollar processing fee and two forms of identification. No cash refunds for non-winners. All wardrobe expenses (needle-brushes, trim, etcetera) are the sole responsibility of the contestant. We reserve the right to remove any participant from the contest should they not smile enough during the pageant preliminaries. Any questions?" With that, the Pageant Lady raced away to deal with other office matters.

Julie inspected the thick forms in her hand, and then put them all into her backpack. A glint of light caught the corner of her eye. There it was. Shockingly close, the crown she needed sparkled on a large blue velvet pillow.

She knew it was magical, but in person it was more than she could ever have imagined. It was in the shape of a large five-pointed star. Covering the star-shaped tiara, clusters of rhinestones were attached around precious and semiprecious stones - amethyst, rubies, pearls, and emeralds. Whether they were real or not made no difference to the awestruck Julie. It was a mesmerizing vision. Unable to control the trance the crown had put her in, she reached forward to touch it. It was lighter than she thought. Holding it in her hands, she felt powerless to fight the urge to place it on her head. So she did. It fit perfectly on the top of her tree-shaped head.

Julie closed her eyes. A sparkling swirl of magical colors floated through her imagination. A whirl of pretty music, wind, snow, all spinning. She was completely captivated. "I wish, I wish..."

The music stopped dead. Julie opened her eyes to see if her world had been reversed. Staring directly at her, nose to nose, was a furious looking Ms. Canadia Hemlock. The Pageant Lady was burning mad.

75

"Your little brother is licking my coffee table!"

That he was. Julie could see him across the office kneeling down to taste the candy furniture.

"Brian!"

Brian laughed as usual sticking out his candy-colored tongue.

"Oh, one other thing. The crown only works for pageant winners!" Ms. Hemlock snatched the bejeweled tiara off Julie's head and placed it back onto the velvet pillow. "Gettit? Gottit? Good! Go! Next problem!" And she was off again.

Julie followed. "Please, I need a wish. It's an emergency."

Before Julie could explain, a pageant assistant poked in his head to interrupt. This was little Ronnie Barkwood. Dedicated and pesky at the same time, Ronnie Barkwood had a way of nagging that reminded one of a dripping faucet. His persistence was quiet and steady. "Um… Ms. Hemlock… we have another emergency. Have you decided who will be the emcee this year?"

ELMA WOOD

OAKANNA
ACORN

"No Ronald. I have not yet made my decision."

In his meek voice he persisted. "I've been practicing. Listen! 'Good evening Ladies and Trees.'"

"Not now, Ronald."

"'I will be your Master of Ceremonies, Ronnie Barkwood.'"

"Not now, Ronald!"

Refusing to give up, he continued. "'I have a joke that will make everybody laugh, too.'"

Having reached the limit of her patience with the determined little shrub of a tree helper, Ms. Hemlock yelled with the steamy power of a tugboat foghorn. "NOT NOW RONALD! Is this your emergency?"

"Um… no. Several members of the Junior Leaf are in the front office."

Flustered and overwhelmed with the many daily surprises, Ms. Hemlock said almost wearily, "Come pageant time, everything is an emergency."

A flurry of complaining could be heard at the front registration desk. A veritable clump of gnarly characters loudly demanded answers.

SILVERA BIRCH

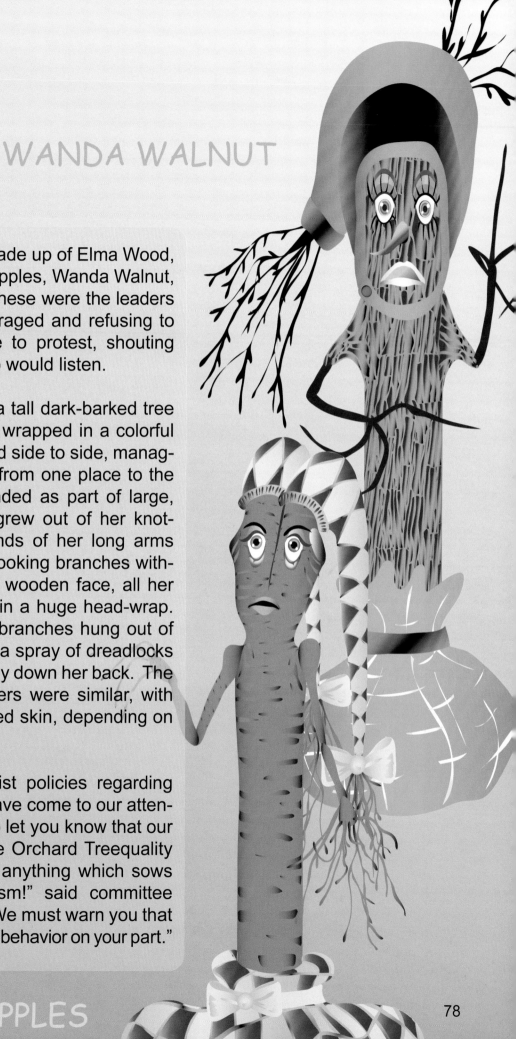

WANDA WALNUT

The group was made up of Elma Wood, Silvera Birch, Crabby Apples, Wanda Walnut, and Oakanna Acorn. These were the leaders of the Junior Leaf. Enraged and refusing to leave, they were there to protest, shouting their opinions to all who would listen.

Elma Wood was a tall dark-barked tree lady whose roots were wrapped in a colorful canvas ball. She shifted side to side, managing somehow to move from one place to the other. Her arms extended as part of large, forking branches that grew out of her knotted shoulders. The ends of her long arms were the tips of wispy looking branches without leaves. Above her wooden face, all her branches were tied up in a huge head-wrap. The leafless cluster of branches hung out of the top of her turban in a spray of dreadlocks that cascaded all the way down her back. The rest of the Junior Leafers were similar, with various shades of barked skin, depending on their own tree variety.

"Your uninclusionist policies regarding pageant participation have come to our attention. And we are here to let you know that our little sub-committee, the Orchard Treequality Patrol, will not tolerate anything which sows the seeds of separatism!" said committee chair Wanda Walnut. "We must warn you that we will root out any unfair behavior on your part."

CRABBY APPLES

78

"Totally unfair!" shouted Elma Wood.

"This year of all years!" added Crabby Apples.

The thoughts of Silvera Birch were not kept secret either. "With television crews everywhere!"

All the Junior Leafers began to chant together:

Treequality! Treequality! We want in!
Treequality! Treequality! We want in!

Ms. Hemlock, not willing to be bullied into a situation that she did not like, planted herself firmly and stood her ground. She spoke with crisp directness. "I… do not… make… the rules… ladies."

"I thought you wrote the book." Julie was puzzled.

"Yeah, she wrote the book!" Brian proclaimed.

Under her breath, Ms. Hemlock tried to get the children out of this. "Children you are not helping." Making a bold statement of fact, she continued. "This is a winter pageant. For evergreens only."

WE WANT IN
WE WANT IN
WE WANT IN
WE WANT IN
WE WANT IN
WE WANT IN
WE WANT IN

Oakanna Acorn pushed her way to the front of the desk and stared directly into Ms. Hemlock's large blue-green eyes. "We have just as much beauty and poise as any common Needled Nelly in the forest!"

For years this debate had existed. Ms. Hemlock felt that, as the pageant founder, she had the right to do it her way. And the Junior Leafers felt that, being such a huge annual event endorsed by the townspeople, the pageant should be open to all.

"I've said it before and I will say it again. If the Junior Leaf Losers want to be in a pageant, I suggest you get together, pick a month, have a parade in the parking lot behind the Sugar Deli 24-Hour Shop-n-Gas Stop, plop a crown of dandelions on your head and presto, bam-o! It's a pageant. I'll be happy to be one of the judges." Canadia's sarcasm did not impress the Junior Leaf.

"The time has come to take a stand! Treequality! We won't give in!"
The argument roared out of control, so much so that Ms. Hemlock called the Candy Cops and requested that they come by to remove her unwanted guests. At that, Julie and Brian quietly left. After all, they still had a list of errands to run.

The end of Chapter Six

Chapter Seven: Trim 'n Tinsel

Back on the street, crazy looking townspeople were in the midst of daily life here in Gingertown. Julie pulled out the note to see what was next.

"I want a wish, too!" nagged Brian.

"Jodi promised me that after she won she'd give me the crown and the wishes. Not you!" said Julie.

"I want a wish! I want a wish!" shouted Brian, relentlessly. Candy people were beginning to stare.

"Cut it out, Brian!" ordered Julie.

"I…WANT…A…WISH!" screamed Brian at the top of his lungs.

Everyone on the street had stopped dead and was now staring directly at them. Julie could see she would have to make a concession. "All right, already, you little brat!" *When* Jodi wins the pageant, and *when* she gives me the crown, and when I have made all the wishes I need to make, *then* I will give you a wish, okay?"

"Okay," said Brian. And with that, he turned suddenly and dashed ahead down the street toward the Petit Four Pet Store. Julie raced to catch him. When she caught up to Brian, he was standing in front of the little storefront, transfixed. It was impossible not to look at all the cute little candy creatures in the window.

"I want a snow slush-puppy for Christmas." Brian tapped on the glass to get the little guys to wag their tails.

"Oh, look… over here. I want a cocoa bunny." Julie was all smiles seeing the hopping and twitching little chocolate rabbits.

The door to the store opened. Colorful customers came out holding a candy cane cage. In it was a bird.

"What kind of bird is it?" asked Julie.

CHOCOLATE CHIP GUPPIES

GINGERSNAP GERBILS

CARMEL NUT TURTLES

LICORICE LIZARDS

The proud new owners replied, "This is a peppermint parakeet." The little bird chirped.

"Oh look how pretty he is," cooed Julie.

Brian, seeing an opportunity to be out of Julie's sight, ran into the store. Julie followed him. Once inside, they were greeted by an array of sweet smells, not at all like the odors in ordinary pet stores. The sound of peeping birds, barking puppies, and mewling kittens combined into an orchestra. It seemed as if they were all singing a song together.

In the front of each pet for purchase, the clearly printed name of its species was placed. Julie followed along, reading the names out loud. "Chocolate Chip Guppies, Gingersnap Gerbils, Caramel Nut Turtles, Licorice Lizards. Marshmallow Guinea Pigs, Neapolitan Angel Fish, Truffle Shelled Snails, Toasted Coconut Spiders. Molasses Monkeys, Bubblegum Blow Fish, Jellyroll Discus Fish, Two-Tone Taffy Goldfish, Gumdrop Finches. Sour Lemon Canaries, Green Gummy Garden Snakes." The winding path through this amazing menagerie led Julie right to Brian. He was where he always could be found in any pet store - standing in front of the fish.

MOLASSES MONKEYS

BUBBLEGUM BLOW FISH

JELLYROLL DISCUS FISH

TWO TONE TAFFY GOLDFISH

MARSHMALLOW GUINEA PIGS

NEAPOLITAN ANGEL FISH

TRUFFEL SHELLED SNAILS

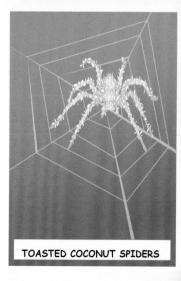

TOASTED COCONUT SPIDERS

"I want a fish," demanded Brian.

"I just gave you a wish, and now you want a fish, too?" reprimanded Julie.

"This is my favorite! The Raspberry-Red Sweetish Gummy Fish. Gramma said I could have one."

Julie was about to disagree. Before she could, Brian pulled out a second note from Gramma. Julie read it. He was telling the truth. This was rare. So Julie waited while Brian picked out a fish. He pointed to the special one that he liked in the corner of the aquarium. The pet store clerk netted up the little fish.

Outside the store, holding up the plastic bag while examining his new little friend, Brian was content.

"Are you happy now?"

"Yes." Brian made fish lips at Julie.

Referring to her own note, Julie followed the next set of instructions.

84

GUMDROP FINCHES

SOUR LEMON CANARIES

GREEN GUMMY GARDEN SNAKES

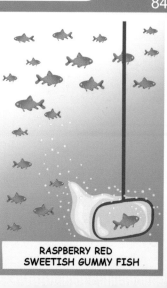

RASPBERRY RED
SWEETISH GUMMY FISH

There it was, just as Gramma had written.

The front door to the shop was actually on the corner. It was a very, very, very small shop, not much bigger than the sled bus shack. Up the front three steps they went. A sign in the glass door had printed on it, "Good things come in small shops." A bell jingled when the door was pulled open, as Julie and Brian entered. The large counter was practically on top of them. There was barely room for them to stand. And not a sparkle or a button anywhere. Julie wondered if maybe this shop was no longer in business. A draped fabric lined the dark wall behind the counter. The two children waited for a few moments in silence. Then, just as they were about to leave, three green faces peeked out from behind the curtain. They were people-shaped faces.

In unison, all three spoke with British accents. "May we help you?"

They came out from behind the covered wall. Julie had been mistaken. These were trees. Topiary trees. Their tops had been clipped into smooth shapes with hairdos to match. There were two ladies, one tall and thin with a high hairstyle, and one short and rounder with a wide face and an even wider hairdo that flipped up on one side into a large curl upon her head. The man tree wore a simple red silk vest with a little white bow tie. The tall slim tree had on a ruffled bib apron and the stout round tree had a waisted apron with pockets in front. These were the owner and his two daughters.

Mr. Topiary spoke first. "Children are not allowed in our store unless accompanied by an adult."

"As you can imagine, in a store as fine as ours, there are many breakables," the tall daughter warned.

What was strange about this statement was that there was not a single item for sale in sight.

The short rounder daughter spoke next. "And little boys are especially suspicious in stores with so much to touch and get dirty, right father?"

"Especially dirty," agreed the father.

Before Julie or Brian could utter a peep or sigh, all three shop attendants leaned over the top of the counter and with woody pointed, white glove covered fingers, all three tapped on a printed sign that was attached to the front of the counter. It was directly in front of the two little shoppers. The three proprietors recited it out loud as a matter of roate. "No children allowed without adult supervision or responsible guardian. No exceptions."

Then Papa Topiary moved in even closer to the two little visitors. "Where are your parents?"

Before Julie could open her very dry and nervous lips, Brian blurted out a response. "They went to Venice-Hula."

Looking perplexed and puzzled by this very curious blurt, the three Topiaries befuddled to one another. "Venice-Hula? What is a Venice-Hula? Where was a Venice-Hula?" Instantly they lifted up a shining planetary globe from under their large counter. Together the three green inspectors quickly eyeballed the entire model with "hmm's and mmm's" of doubt.

Julie feeling that more information was needed to help solve this investigation of sorts spoke. "They went on a vacation."

Again without invitation Brian added, "Yeah, without us. 'Cause Julie never stops fighting with me an' she has tantrums all the time. An' she picks her nose when she thinks nobody is looking."

Trying not to blast her little brother while at the same time boiling over, Julie pulled on the back of Brian's scarf. "Stop lying!"

Being over dramatic Brian added a melodramatic flair with fake tears. "Wahhh. You hurt me. She always hurts me and pinches me. And she tells me I'm a brat all the time."

"You are a brat all the time!"

Eye rolls and lip squenching expressions of aggravation consumed the Topiaries. For this type of behavior was not tolerated here at Trim 'n Tinsel. They nodded in unison as to the next course of action they would follow to flatten the uncomfortable situation that was brewing before them.

At that same moment the taller sister leaped to the door to open it up.

Papa Topiary bent over, "Thank you for shopping. You are free to leave now."

In a confused rustle of activity the two crying and complaining children silently turned to exit.

"That's it," said the taller sister. A sinister grin of manipulation was had by her. "The park is so lovely today. It's just down the street. Have a nice day. And here, for each of you a complimentary sucker from Trim 'n Tinsel."

Brian took a single step out the door. After one sloppy lick of the colorful treat he stopped and made an icky face. "Hey this isn't even a real sucker. It tastes like wax paper and crayons."

"Yes, those are our special 'Decorative' treats. Pretty aren't they?" smiled the taller sister with a hint of sarcastic twinkle in her eyes.

Julie momentarily stopped and yanked Brian's scarf, pulling him back into the shop. She remembered what it was they were there for and spoke up. "We have a note."

"Hmm?" All three proprietors looked at one another. With continued suspicion, they waited for more information.

Julie put the note up on the counter for them to read. "It's from my grandmother. My Gramma signed it too."

A large magnifying glass was brought out from under the counter. They inspected the note as if it were a possible forgery. "The handwriting is most definitely that of an adult. Yes, yes, yes, uh huh." All three topiaries read the last lines together aloud:

Love, Gramma - P.S. Have fun!

"Fun? Father! She thinks that shopping is fun."

"Yes, I also question her motives for coming into our store, Papa," said the stout daughter pointing at Julie. "She could be one of… them."

"But she does have the letter," said the tall topiary sister.

"*We* were not allowed to go into a store by ourselves until we were 12, right Papa?"

"Let alone with such a huge responsibility," declared Mr. Topiary.

The three shop owners moved in closer towards Brian, speaking as one. "And with a fish!"

"His name is Brian." Julie replied.

"The fish?" All three had misunderstood Julie.

"A fish named Brian? I've heard of a fish named Charles, but never Brian." A confused and animated conversation ensued among the topiaries.

"No! *I'm* Brian. And my fish's name is…"

The anticipation of what Brian was to call his new little pet intrigued everyone. Even the fish moved closer to the edge of the plastic to hear his new name. Brian thought and thought, and in a blurt, he said it: "Bottle Cap!" The little fish swam in fast circles.

Puzzled and confused, thinking that perhaps this little tree boy-child might not have the cultural breeding that the Topiaries were accustomed to, all three trees repeated the name in a snobbish manner. "Bottle Cap? How terribly…"

"Strange." Julie finished their thought aloud. "My little brother is not normal."

"I'm glad she said it first," commented the tall sister.

"It must be from the parents' lack of discipline," said the shorter sister.

Brian topped off his boyish behavior by licking the plastic fish bag. The proprietors were appalled.

Julie, noticing once again the lack of merchandise in the store, decided to ask a question. "Where do you keep all of your stuff to buy? I mean, in such a small shop?"

As if having been intentionally insulted, the Topiaries quickly moved to either side of Julie and Brian. A cloak of secrecy fell on the space. The window blinds were lowered. The front door was locked. The lights were dimmed. Whispery questions were asked of the two little shoppers.

"That depends. Are you a 'No thank you, just looking?'"

"An' I'll come back after I've thought about it?'"

"Are you planning to 'Buy it, bring it back after 30 days without a receipt, and cause a scene?'"

"Charge with bad credit?"

"A rubber check passer?"

"'Can't make up my mind,' waste our time type? Hmmm?"

"Or, *perhaps*, a secret shopping spy from Baubles 'R Best?"

All three Topiaries peeked mysteriously out the mini-blinds on the front door window of the little shop, looking diagonally across the street. Julie and Brian joined them.

There, on the opposite corner, sat another little shop similar to Trim 'n Tinsel. It bore a small sign that read "Baubles 'R Best." Peering through mini-blinds from within the other store were the Baubles 'R Best storeowners, who were also spying. The Baubles employees quickly closed the blinds when they saw the Trim 'n Tinsel people looking back at them.

Julie felt she had to clarify herself, "No, I am a customer that wants to buy. Really, I do."

The Topiaries had a quick conference, and returned with a new approach. Without her realizing it, they swiftly webbed wires and electrodes onto Brian and Julie. The two little trees were a mass of wires. Microphones were shoved into their faces just under their mouths.

"Please read the large sign behind the counter." The shorter sister held up a boldly printed card. "It's for our customer file."

Under the counter, out of sight from the mistrusted duo, a large machine with a detector graph was unveiled. All three Topiaries watched.

Doing as she was asked, as a matter of reflex, Julie first read the cards to herself. She felt strangely guilty, as if she were being punished for something she didn't do. This was so unfair to accuse here of anything just because she was a child.

"Read the card dear… It's our standard customer entrance policy for anyone who stands lower than this line." The taller sister quickly marked a chalk line just above Julie's head on the entrance doorframe.

"Even the Fluffer-nutter child of the mayor himself, had to take the test." Commented the shorter sister.

"And what a set of sticky fingers they had. Touching everything." Papa Topiary was in the midst of a mini flashback of horror as he recounted the aggravation that he had on that particular day. "And holding and squeezing, Fluffer-nutter schmuck everywhere. What a mess. What a mess."

Julie read aloud. "I will not steal. I want to buy. I am not a spy."

The detector graph glowed green.

A sense of joyous relief filled the tiny room. The customer test had been passed! No longer suspicious of the intentions of the little shoppers, the Topiaries were now completely cordial.

"That's what we like to hear."

The counter unfolded. Under it, a silver metal shopping cart with over-sized wheels was revealed. The Topiaries quickly put Julie and Brian into it. Goggles were placed on all. With a flick of several switches located on the sides of the Topiaries' roller skate shoes, all three shopkeepers' feet lit up. The thick curtain was slowly pulled back. Behind it lay a dark open doorway.

"Are we ready?"

"Ready."

Click, click, click, click… click, click, click, click… Blast!

Rocketing into the dark opening, the cart was propelled by the power roller-skates. Down, down, down it went. Into the dark space they plummeted. Faster and faster they went. Colorful lights flashed. Air rushed through Julie's and Brian's needles. Ahead Julie could see the opening. Closer, and faster, and closer and faster - it was great, laughing fun. Slowing to a swift, smooth stop, the cart arrived in the underground Trim 'n Tinsel shopping caverns.

"This used to be our great grand daddy's silver mine. Or so he thought. It never produced enough silver to make a single strand of tinsel. So we turned it into our Secret Shoppers Club."

"You must promise that you will never tell the proprietors of Baubles 'R Best just what we have down here."

"We won't. We promise!" Julie was all excited. "How big is it?"

"Oh, about 7 miles or so, if you include all the crawl spaces." Father Topiary was not nearly so gruff as he had first appeared. Neither were his daughters.

I guess you can't judge a person until you get to know them. Thought Julie. It was a regular phrase that Grampa always used.

The two children sat happily in the cart as the Topiary sisters pushed them up and down the many aisles.

"We have silks. We have wool. We have cotton, crepe and poly. We have beads. We have pearls. And stones that can be set, sewn or glued."

"We also have laces, and fringes, and sneakers with polka dot green splotches."

"How many different colors of glitter do you have?" inquired Julie.

The cart was quickly rolled to a specific merchandise isle. The tall sister spoke up, "Seven hundred forty-three different shades, to be exact."

Julie gasped. "How do I choose? I could be here for days."

The two sisters laughed. "Actually, you could be here for months. We have down here a small camp of indecisive shoppers that still haven't made up their mind on wallpaper samples." The two sisters rolled past the shoppers that they spoke of and waved. "Hello Miss Mulberry and Miss Rootwood." The two undecided shoppers were surrounded by piles and piles of large books with wallpaper samples from all over the world.

"I don't have months to choose. I only have until the last sled bus leaves town tonight. How will I know I didn't miss the right choice, or forget something truly important?" Julie was now curiously stumped.

The cart was rolled up to the main counter. There stood Mr. Topiary. "At Trim 'n Tinsel we have various selling policies. For an additional $2.31, a personal shopper may choose the most sumptuous, delicious, radiant, items we have… within your financial means and budgetary limits, that is."

"Or if you like, we have the Merchandise Picks You plan."

A drawer in the counter opened. From inside it, little talking trinkets all cried in high-pitched voices, "Take us home. Pick me. I'm pretty, pick me."

The drawer closed shut.

"Due to your limited time schedule, limited experience, and budgetary limits, we have selected a plan for you." An envelope got passed from tree to tree until it reached Mr. Topiary. A recording of a drum roll and cymbal crash, followed by musical fanfares and cheering crowds was played. Down from the ceiling, balloons and streamers had turned this into a party. With great ceremony, Mr. Topiary slowly opened the envelope. "The Wheel Of Merchandise plan!"

"Yea! We won! We Won!" Without even really knowing what had just happened, Brian was cheering wildly.

Julie, being a little more inquisitive, asked, "How does it work?"

"You simply spin the wheel. And whatever it lands on, that's what you buy! We can assure you that every item is of the best possible quality."

A large game-show-wheel with hundreds of choices descended from the cavernous ceiling of the former mine. Julie noticed it was all numbers, no words. Before she could get out of the cart, Brian had already jumped out and was ready to spin the wheel.

"I want to spin it!" He shouted. Then with a big arm tug, he pulled the wheel as hard as he could. Round and round it went. *Tic, tic, tic, tic, tic, tic, tic.* It stopped.

Not knowing just what had just been purchased, off raced the shorter sister to get it. "Isle 9, shelf 27, item Number… 6."

Then Julie spun the wheel. Whatever she wound up buying - it didn't really matter, because this was so much fun. How could she possibly go wrong, with all the wonderful choices here at Trim 'n Tinsel?

The end of Chapter Seven

Chapter Eight: Competitive Spirit

"You've got to be kidding. You got me black?!" Jodi had been quite anxious to see just what her crazy little fashion-designing sister had bought at Trim 'n Tinsel. Placing the large shopping bag on her bed, she looked inside. "Black? For a Christmas tree pageant? Whoever heard of black on a Christmas tree?"

Defending her bag of items, Julie said, "It's very… fashion-forward."

Jodi continued to inspect the contents. "And rickrack? Rickrack trim went out with designer pine-jeans and needle teasing. Carnation floral spray? What do you think I am, a prom corsage? I am going to look like a freak!" Jodi was having a ranting fit. The more she analyzed the mixed and matched items Julie had brought home, the more upset she became.

Ida Mae knew it wasn't always the materials, but how they were put together that mattered. She offered Julie positive encouragement. "Julie, you did a wonderfully creative job. When we mix my old with your new, who knows what we will come up with?"

"Thanks Gramma."

Brian was currently in his room, far away from this conversation. He was about to put his Raspberry Red Sweetish Gummy Fish into his fish tank. Brian held Bottle Cap in the palm of his mitten, petting him gently, as Tiger Lily sat next to the aquarium, watching intently.

"Look, Tiger Lily, you have a new little gummy brother."

"Meow?" Tiger Lily moved in for a closer inspection.

"Look, but don't touch!" said Brian, who himself could not resist licking the tasty little candy fellow before tossing him in the tank.

"Meow!" Brian had done what Tiger Lily wanted to do, but couldn't. She continued to watch Bottle Cap swim back and forth in his new home as her bushy green tail whipped back and forth almost in unison.

Julie and Gramma went downstairs to make a master plan of all the things that needed to be done. A creative spirit filled the cozy winter farmhouse.

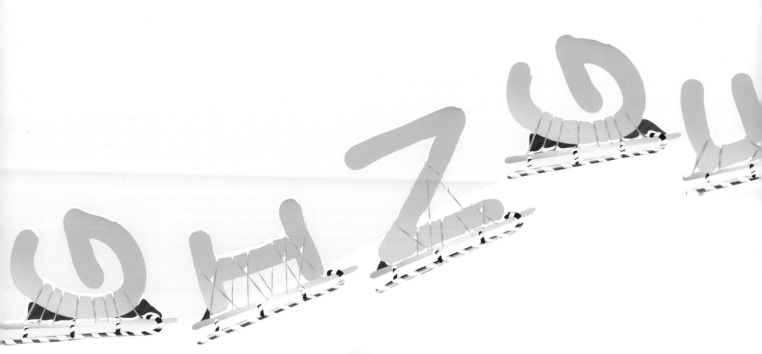

There were only eight days left until Christmas, and only seven days left to prepare for the pageant.

Over the next few days, Jodi became stronger and stronger, holding up the tea-cups with ever-growing grace and ease. Her confidence level soon rose to that of a fierce pageant contestant. She could recite practically all the tongue twisters written in Canadia's pageant guide. Sharp and ready to stand tall with perfect posture, it was finally time to experiment with fashions.

Julie and her grandmother had a vision of how wonderful Jodi could look. They had diagrams and sketches all over the house. But before the final decision, they tested a variety of combinations on her. It was hard to make a skinny stick of a tree into a Covertree model. They removed her glasses, which was a huge improvement, but then she tripped into everything. They added branch weaves to her figure. This would have been a viable solution if only they didn't fall off whenever she turned around too quickly. Various spray colors were tested to give her a magic glow, but it seemed like everything made her itch. Still, they moved on, eliminating what didn't work and focusing on what did.

Redda gossiped to all who would listen, filling everyone in on every little detail concerning the new TV people in town. "Oh did you see the television crew? They have cameras, and trucks, and sound equipment, and photographers! I would be so happy to let them all know the history of the pageant. I could show them my red garland dress. It's a real collectible."

Putting their best faces forward was on the minds of all the civic-minded residents of Gingertown. Every little shop, café, office, and hotel cleaned and primped. The most luscious and cherished holiday decorations were hung to celebrate the big event.

Giant oversized letters standing 20-feet high were created. Slowly, they were sledded up to the huge hill, which overlooked the little town. Visible to all the town's residents and guests, GINGERTOWN was spelled out in shocking lime green letters. Shortly after the sign had been erected, the giant green "G", for some odd reason, slipped from its foundation. It appeared that the bolts used to hold it in place had not been secured properly. No one was hurt, but what looked at first to be an easy job became a day filled with ongoing problems. Once it was completely reinstalled without fear of future collapse, all the townspeople cheered. The visibility of the shocking lime green sign in contrast to the snow-frosting covered hill especially delighted the television camera crews. At night, all the letters glowed.

To welcome the many tourists and reporters from all over the land, a huge banner was made and stretched across Main Street. "Welcome, World, to the Gingertown Christmas Eve Pageant."

A crowd of gawkers gathered to watch the workmen install the banner. Slowly they strung cables across the road to support the sign. Higher and higher it was lifted. Mixed in among the cheering crowd was one dissatisfied individual. Everyone is so happy, thought a negative onlooker. *Why? Why was everyone so glad to welcome the world?*

Bitter and uncaring, the negative white-gloved naysayer pulled out a sharpened knife. And when no one was looking… *Slash!* The tension cable that took so long to mount snapped. Down fell the sign. Coincidentally, the sled bus, making its regular rounds, was just under the sign at that very moment. Or was it a coincidence? The timing was just too perfect.

First, the sign fell on Doug. Then… *Crash!* Having no clear vision, Doug plowed right into a souvenir tent. A single gingerman worker was left dangling from the torn sign, waiting for help. The damage was done, but no one quite knew just how or why. "Accidents happen all the time," they all said, for a deliberate act of sabotage wasn't even a thought here in Gingertown.

Noticing this incident from their window, Ms. Hemlock and her trusty treesistant little Ronnie Barkwood were heavily involved with yet more pageant matters.

"All signed?"

"Yes ma'am."

"Properly addressed?"

"Yes ma'am."

"Has the list been checked and double checked and triple checked?"

"Yes ma'am."

A grand proclamation was then made by Ms. Hemlock, "Open the window."

"Ahh, Ms. Hemlock, have you made your decision yet? About the… uhh… master of ceremonies person?"

"Yes. I'm sorry to say Ronald that because the pageant will be televised this year, the sponsors have selected a professional. Now open the window."

"But you said that this would be my year to emcee the pageant. Listen, I can be very charming. 'Good evening Ladies and Trees. I will be your Master of Ceremonies.'"

Ronnie Barkwood had been practicing for his debut as pageant emcee all year. And he had had a good shot at finally getting to do it. That was, until it was announced that the program would be televised. Ronnie wanted it so bad, he just didn't want to believe that he had been replaced.

"Not now, Ronald." Ms. Hemlock, though she loved her pesky little treesistant, was losing her patience.

Ronnie continued trying to prove to her that he could do it. "'Tonight we will have a forest of beauties here on this stage.' Do you like the forest part? That's supposed to be a joke."

"Not now, Ronald! Open the window!"

Pushing with all his might, the frail little fellow grunted and hummed while struggling with the window frame, which was frozen shut with snow frosting. Under his breath, he complained to himself. "It's not fair. I can be just as charming as some Candywood phony." Using his anger, he was able to break through the snow frosting. "Up… up… and up!"

The window now stood wide open. Ms. Hemlock pulled a large golden cord untying the giant mailing sack that had been positioned under the sill. Out rushed a flipping, flapping, fluttering swarm of butterflygrams. Racing up into the sky like a flock of birds, the anxious little note-carriers created a spectacle for all the passing folk, as the second floor window from which they were released faced the town square. The residents of Gingertown began to shout their approval.

"I hope I get one!"

"Look, one is landing on me!"

"And look over there. One just landed on that mail box… and another one on that little girl!"

These were no ordinary butterflies, but giant, oversized, sugar-frosted butterfly grams. With wings the size of Ping-Pong paddles, each one was a sparkling, glimmering kaleidoscope of delicate patterns. Carefully inscribed on the wings of each was an invitation to the annual Pre-Pageant High Tea. No one knew just how the magical little note carriers came to be, or how Ms. Hemlock trained them to find whomever they were addressed to. It was yet another little secret that made living in Gingertown wonderful. The excitement was a clear reminder that the holidays had officially begun.

"The butterflygrams are free! The butterflygrams are free!" cheered everyone in the town.

Crabby Apples and her greenless friends saw the spectacle as well. Reaching up in a woody, leafless snatch, Crabby yanked one of the little miracles from the winter sky. "Humph! We never get invited!" she declared.

Flitting off into the beyond, one butterflygram in particular headed up over the hills, past the gumdrop forests, over the little sled bus stop, and landed right on the front door of the Needles' farmhouse.

Jodi read the invitation aloud. "To Miss Jodi Needles. You are graciously invited to the Pre-Pageant High Tea, as are family members of your choice. This gathering will take place at the Wedding Cake Café at twelve noon on December 22nd. Please be prompt. Proper Wedding Cake Café attire required. Please RSVP without delay."

"Are we going?" Julie was excited.

"Of course, we're going!" exclaimed Gramma. "We're all going. And hopefully your Grampa Joe will be back in time to attend as well."

"What's a 'High Tea?'" asked Julie.

A girlish glint filled Ida Mae's eye. Just thinking about a High Tea brought back memories for her. "High Tea is a wonderful afternoon party. It's not quite lunch or dinner. The host of a High Tea usually serves tiny little sandwiches no bigger than a cracker and wonderful fancy little sweet creations. And, of course, delicious tea blends from all over the world. Everyone who attends always seems to act with politeness and be on their very best behavior. I don't know why exactly, but for some puzzling reason High Tea and politeness go hand in hand."

Julie had come up with the perfect analogy. "High Tea and politeness, it's like peanut butter and jelly."

Jodi held the fluttering butterfly gram flat and wrote her acceptance on the wing with a candy colored marker.

"I want to do it. I want to do it!" Brian then picked up the giant butterfly and carried it to the front porch. He was all smiles as he lifted his mitten covered tree limbs. Up into the sky the flitting creature traveled back to the pageant office like a homing pigeon.

"My goodness, I completely forgot about the tea," said Ida Mae. "We've been so consumed getting Jodi ready for the contest."

The end of Chapter Eight

Chapter Nine: Pageant Polite

A fluffy powdered-sugar snowfall added the right amount of holiday spirit to the day of the High Tea. Gingertown was alive with shoppers and residents from the outer farm regions.

The famous eatery, which was situated quite perfectly between the Butter Cream Hotel and a colorfully built row of cookie townhouses, was shaped like a four-tiered cake. Covering the circular building was a thick layer of misty pink stucco frosting. On each roof level of the quaint structure, giant white candle torch lights flickered. This was no ordinary fast food, chocolate-hotdog-on-a lemon-meringue-bun snack house, according to the loyal patrons, but the fanciest restaurant in town.

It was a sight to behold, as the guests, standing in line on the circular Wedding Cake Café carpet, had all arrived dressed in proper attire. This meant that each patron had a choice of being either a bride, a groom, a flower seedling, or an usher. No exceptions.

Jodi was wearing a headdress with a long train made out of an old lace tablecloth. Her grandmother had on a headdress and train made from her dining room drapes, and Julie was wearing a miniature bride's outfit made from fabric scraps left over from Ida Mae's sewing projects. Each carried a small bouquet of candy flowers. Brian held a satin couch pillow with a little satin tie to match. Grampa Joe had returned with Great Aunt Sylvia, and they too were dressed in the finest wedding attire Ida Mae could whip up on such short notice. Standing behind them, in front of them and every which way they looked were brides, brides, and more brides. Even Ms. Hemlock and Little Ronnie Barkwood were dressed in wedding attire.

As each guest entered the main door of the event space, the sound of wedding bells and pipe organs could be heard.

Making her grand entrance (always wanting to be the center of attention) and getting into the spirit of the party, Redda sang the Wedding March aloud as she moved one step at a time across the open dance floor. "Da, da, da da… Da, da, da da…"

Dressed as a giant flower seedling, Redda tossed sugar rose petals to all. And following behind Redda, dressed in full bridal gowns and veils, was her granddaughter La Cona and Cypress Limb.

"Oh that Redda!" laughed everyone in the room.

"Joe, how dashing you look in your groom outfit," complimented Redda. "How lovely everyone looks. And Sylvia, we haven't seen you since the last snow blizzard. What wonderful brides you all make. I'd like you all to meet my granddaughter La Cona, and her friend Cypress Limb."

"She's from Kentucky," blurted out Brian.

"Very good Brian," answered Cypress. "Why, you are a sharp little sapling. I'll have to keep a special eye on you!" Cypress Limb reached down to give Brian an especially hard squeeze on his cheek needles.

The seating arrangement placed Brian next to Cypress and Jodi next to La Cona.

"Oh look, one seat left for me. I must be the head of the table," Redda laughed with a self-praising smile.

On every plate was a pattern of gold and silver doves. The napkins were made of lace and the tablecloth felt like a silk ball gown. The luxury of this event would surely last in Julie's mind for as long as she lived.

Miniature sandwiches and cookies were being placed in the center of the grand table setting by the café wait staff. Brian, no-mannered brat that he always was, stuffed his face with cookie sandwiches. He smiled at Cypress Limb with blue frosting-covered teeth. She smiled back, secretly, with blue icing in her mouth too. Brian giggled. Meanwhile, Grampa Joe and Ida Mae caught up on the latest family news with Great Aunt Sylvia.

Redda kicked off the conversation. "Ida, I love what you've done with your old drapes and table cloth. Didn't you wear the same drapes in '61? Hmm? That was the year I won."

"I always thought you did it in '59," answered Ida Mae with a sweet smile.

"Oh no dear, I'm not as old as you are, it was in '61. And if you remember I did it in..."

"A red garland and silver stars evening gown." Before Redda could finish another backhanded remark, Great Aunt Sylvia finished it for her. "I was sitting in the front row, dear. And yes, those are the same drapes and lace Ida Mae wore in '61. They were my mother's drapes and tablecloth. Aren't they still as lovely as ever? Oh I remember it as clear as if it were yesterday."

Great Aunt Sylvia never forgot a thing. And if she could help it, she wasn't going to let Redda twist the conversation into a series of cutting remarks.

"And I also remember what a sweet little flower seedling you made at my wedding oh so many years ago Redda. There was little Ida Mae, little Joseph and, little Redda."

"Sylvia, Sylvia, you don't have to tell that old story again." Redda tried to get Great Aunt Sylvia to change the subject, but it was not going to happen.

"Redda, I never tire of telling my story... as much as you never tire of telling yours." Great Aunt Sylvia lifted her needled eyebrows with a pursed-lipped smile.

"What story?" This was one the children had never heard.

The family tale became very real to all, as Great Aunt Sylvia spoke.

"When I was a young tree about to be married, I was dear friends with Redda's mother. And upon learning that I was to be wed, a matter of confusion took place. For little Ida Mae was to be my flower seedling and little Joseph my ring bearer. Somehow, the communication of who was doing what got all mixed up. Little Redda thought that she was going to become the flower seedling. No matter how hard we tried to convince her that she wasn't the flower seedling, she refused to believe it. Well, to make peace with Redda's mother, I agreed to have two flower seedlings. Later after the ceremony at the reception hall, another drama unfolded for little Redda. She wanted wedding cake. And she wanted it right then and there. I tried to explain to her that dinner hadn't been served yet, and it was always customary to cut the cake after dinner. But no, little Redda had to have cake for dinner or nothing."

Even Cypress Limb was captivated. "So did she get to eat cake for dinner?"

Redda quietly nibbled on a tea sandwich rolling her eyes. The town gossip was getting a dose of her own medicine. "Oh, Sylvia, no one wants to hear about my past."

"Yes we do," declared everyone at the table.

Great Aunt Sylvia continued while looking directly into Redda's eyes. "So she cried and cried and cried herself into a fit. And she cried so hard and for so long… that she wet her root boots."

Brian did what everyone else wanted to. He laughed out loud. "You wet your root boots!" The entire luncheon party snickered, including the waiters that were hovering around the table to overhear the tale.

Great Aunt Sylvia was the one tree who could always get the upper limb when it came to Redda Pinesky. "Oh I remember she ate so many cookies, and so much cake that we thought she was going to explode. She ate, and ate, and ate. Didn't you Redda? And look at her today. I don't think she ever stopped."

"Well, I guess I always did have a sweet tooth. And as they say, nobody is perfect."

Great Aunt Sylvia smiled and sipped her tea. "Exactly."

Redda knew she was in the company of someone who could put her in her place. Redda quietly finished her tea sandwich. And then three or four more.

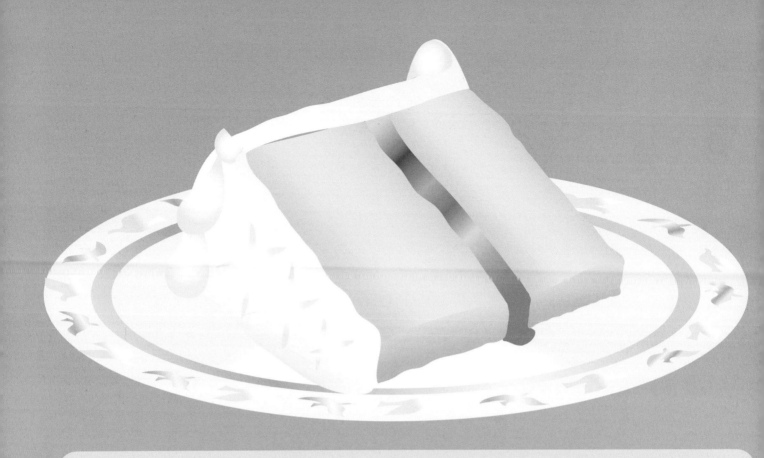

To poke fun, the waiters brought Redda a fresh piece of wedding cake. "Here you go, Mrs. Pinesky. We wouldn't want you to wet your root boots." They laughed, as did Redda, trying not to show her uneasiness.

Knowing how to turn words her way, La Cona came to her grandmother's rescue by diverting the conversation. "How simply chic you look Jodi, in your country lace headpiece and un-pruned branches. I hear that shabby-chic is all the rage in the big cities. City folks can't get enough of peeling paint and rusty old country furniture. I bet if you moved to the big city, they'd put you on the cover of one of those makeover magazines."

Jodi, who had decided not to go overboard with fashion or false branch weaves, looked almost the same as the old Jodi that everyone knew. Her only modification for this High Tea was to wear high root heels, long dinner gloves, and a little red barkstick on her lips.

La Cona's comment was exactly what one might have expected from the granddaughter of Redda. It was polite and cutting at the same time. Jodi knew she was trying to upset her, but she wasn't going to take the bait.

"And once again I must say how proud I am of you, Ida," commented Redda regaining her usual verbal momentum, "encouraging your granddaughter to follow in the footsteps of her nana. And with eyeglasses too! In my day a girl wouldn't have been caught dead in a pageant wearing thick glasses." Redda held up a cup of tea. "Let's hear it for the modern, un-cultivated woman. Free to be a natural beauty."

"Yes it is liberating." commented Jodi. What she politely said was one thing, and what she was thinking was another. Just two minutes alone with that greenhouse phony granddaughter of Redda's, and Jodi would kick the sap out of her. But Jodi had to bite her tongue… if she wanted to play the game. "Thank you, Redda and La Cona, for the lovely words. I'm saving up all my pretty time for the competition." Jodi flut-tered her eyelashes under her glasses to be sweet. Ida Mae, Joe, and Sylvia were proud of her ladylike response.

"Do you have something in your eye?" asked Julie.

Jodi looked to Julie and pinched her under the table while speaking in a frozen, fake smile. "Yes…love."

Julie and Brian giggled.

"Oh I understand where she's coming from," remarked Cypress. "I, too, was once a thicket pine growin' up. But with the discovery of mail order cosmetics, I have reaped the potential of my beauty. All you need, Honey, is a charge card and a paintbrush, and you can be as glamorous as me." The Kentucky visitor smiled a sweet, country smile - with blue icing still on her lips. Cypress was a walking advertisement for too much everything - her false eyelashes, her dry, flaky-looking face foundation, her stiff over-sprayed needles. And yet, somehow this false reality she had adopted for herself was now who she had become. She was the ac-ceptable norm for most, if not all, the pageant entrants.

Jodi realized that Cypress was just another category of the many types of beauty she saw on a daily basis. There was everyday-on-the-street beauty, going-to-school beauty, feeling-pretty-beauty, and now - this overly-modern, overly-fake pageant beauty. Who knew there were so many definitions of pretty?

Julie whispered to Jodi under her breath while they sipped their tea. "Why is everybody being so mean to each other? I thought every-one had to be polite at a High Tea?"

"This is all just part of the game, little sister. It's called pageant polite, or the big psych-out. It's in chapter six of the rules book."

For the first time, Julie was seeing what Jodi had tried to point out to her all along.

The High Tea concluded with announcements. Stepping up to the podium, little Ronnie Barkwood was too short to speak easily into the microphone. In order to be heard, he had to tilt it on a downward angle. "Good evening Ladies... I mean good afternoon Ladies and Trees. I have a joke to…" And before he could tell his High Tea joke, Canadia stepped up to cut him off.

"Thank you, Ronald." He stepped back, feeling rather small. As she spoke, her voice echoed with reverb from the old-fashioned microphone. "Attention… attention contestants, mothers of contestants, friends of contestants, aunts and uncles of contestants, aromatherapy support psychologists for contestants. I am proud to welcome you all. Through the gracious support of our television coordinators, we will be treated to the magic makeover hands of Jose Éclair and his staff of beauty experts."

Jose, a creampuff dessert, stepped forward wearing a cookie cowboy hat. A long ponytail of curly coconut shavings was tied to the back of his head. He was definitely a man of flair.

The crowd applauded. Ms. Hemlock stood next to him, also basking in the praise. "Mr. Éclair and his Gingerbread Salon needle and bark specialists will be backstage to assist you in your transformations." With this, Canadia handed the microphone to Jose.

"Thank you. Thank you. I will have the wonderful honor of finding the innermost filling of each and everyone's beauty potential here. Where else can a cream-filled dessert like myself and his team of gingerbread boy beauty consultants wear wedding veils and corsages without feeling foolish?" They all quickly put on veils in front of the audience. Everyone laughed.

"And to officially end today's High Tea at the luxurious Wedding Cake Café, I will need all the contestants to join me now on the main dance floor," requested Jose.

What was about to happen was a surprise to all. "In the spirit of things, I will toss out my beauty bouquet," he announced. "Whoever catches it will win the door prize - a complete tip-to-root massage at the hands of my wonderful gingerbread makeover beauty boys, and a gift certificate from Gingertown's one and only Sweets Treats Pizza Palace!"

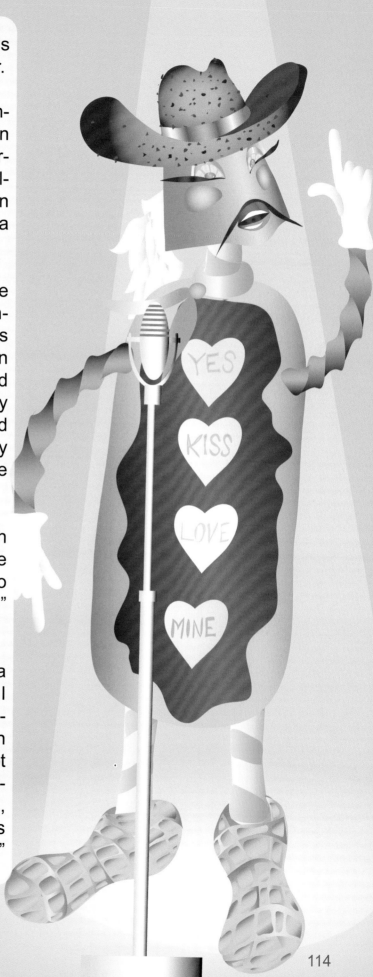

The dance floor quickly filled with the contestants. It was fun to see Jodi as one of them, thought Julie. Standing in between La Cona and Cypress, Jodi felt confident that she was far more the athlete here and could out-jump or out-race both of them. She really didn't want to be massaged or eat Sweet Treat pizza, but catching the bouquet was all about the principle of it.

"One, two and… three!" Jose Éclair tossed the bouquet. Up it went with all eyes watching. Jodi took a step, but before she could take a serious leap she tripped and fell. It felt as though someone had deliberately tripped her. A domino effect of falling timber took place, as most of the girls were all tangled up in their wedding trains.

"I got it! I got it!" La Cona had won.

Still standing with her wedding dress hiked up and her veil wrapped in a turban, she waved to Redda, who was tossing sugar rose petals to all with joy.

Aching to be even more snide with Jodi, La Cona drawled ever so sweetly, "Oh dear me, you must have gotten your high root heels tangled up in your party veil. That happens a lot to trees that normally are accustomed to wearing only rubber root flats. Can I give you a branch up?"

"No thank you, I can do it by myself."

Jodi felt humiliated. Tripping was no big deal. And she really didn't care about winning the bouquet. So why did it bother her so much? Because now she had seen the other side of this contest. She now knew what she was up against. And it was now that she realized she had only two days left to perfect her competitive skills.

The end of Chapter Nine

TICKETS

PARKING

B
A
R
N

Canadia
Hemlock
presents
The first time
ON TELEVISION
A
GINGERTOWN
Christmas
SPECIAL

TICKET
INFORMATION

ORCHESTRA

SOLD OUT

BALCONY

STAGE
DOOR

PAGEANT

ENTRANCE

Chapter Ten: Lights! Camera!

At last, the day of the big contest had arrived. Standing at the backstage entrance to the theater, a crowd waited nervously. Slowly, the big, heavy, pound cake door was pushed open. Greeting the contestants as they entered was Ms. Hemlock's frail little treesistant. Before he could whisper a word, Ronnie was trampled by contestants stampeding to the dressing rooms. The frantic behavior was infectious. Screaming and giddy laughter echoed through the hall. Out front, the glorious Gingertown Barn Theater marquee was all lit up. Big bold neon lights blinked the word "BARN" on and off. Roving searchlights, that had been brought to the little town by the broadcast crews, beamed into the frosty, moist evening sky.

"Get your programs here!" "Buy a little souvenir!" "Balloons for the little ones!" "Get your Tree Time Cola here!" A circus of vendors lined the sidewalk that led up to the theater. Anyone who had anything to sell was out front.

One of the many reporters that swarmed the front of the building was giving a news report to the camera crew. "The Gingertown Barn Theater, or simply 'The Barn' as the younger 'in-crowd' likes to call it, is a grand old structure. At one time, it actually was a barn. But over the years, with modifications and additions, it has grown into a giant community center for all kinds of activities. Movies, dances, parties, conventions, graduations - whenever there is a big event in Gingertown, it takes place here."

The on-looking local residents were proud. Now the world was going to get a glimpse of this cherished old theater, coast-to-coast.

"Inside the Barn, the two-tiered balcony is beginning to fill up with ticket holders. Everybody and anybody who is somebody important is here tonight. Dressed in stylish attire, the audience members seem to be dressed as lavishly, or perhaps even more lavishly, than the young tree-beauties in the pageant," reported a second newscaster, looking down onto the main floor from his perch in the balcony. His image was being monitored on closed-circuit television by the control booth located in the van just outside.

"We have it. The sound levels are great," said the technician. "I bet all of the unlucky local residents who couldn't get seats tonight are at home glued to their sofas eating popcorn and sipping sweet soft drinks. Oh-oh, it's time…"

A drum roll. This was it! The director called the first cue from within the van. "Camera one, camera two, camera three."

The control booth gave the signal. "Five, four, three, two, image now…"

The voiceover announcer spoke from his outside location. "Welcome to the first-ever live broadcast of the Gingertown Christmas Eve Pageant."

"Cut to the aerial shot," yelled the director.

"Looking down from our helicopter coverage, we see the newly-famous glowing green Gingertown hilltop sign. What a sight! Look how beautiful this mountain community is. It's as if the houses are coated in diamonds, glittering in the night. And now we give you our master of ceremonies, Freddie Molasses."

"Freddie on camera one..." The cookie men in the control booth were on top of the director's orders.

"Hello, I am your host for this evening, Freddie Molasses."

The crowd applauded him energetically.

"That's it. Give it up. Give it up. I haven't heard this much yelling since the Lazy Pie Bake Off!" Everyone laughed as Freddie egged them on.

"Oh, look who's laughing there in the judges' row. Limon Sour. What do you say, Limon?"

Limon, a half-lemon, half-lime sour candy celebrity, was his usual sour self. That's why the crowds liked him. "I have only one thing to say. I hope this pageant doesn't suck."

Boos and laughter filled the house.

Freddie, a comical molasses cookie emcee, moved on to the next judge. "And seated next to Mr. Sourpuss, the lovely and ever-yummy Carmella Cashew."

"Thank you Freddie. I will try to be the sweet one on the panel this evening, as I am flanked by a Mr. Sourpuss and a Mr. Jawbreaker."

"And now I don't get an introduction," chimed in the next judge, Candy Jawbreaker.

"Not to worry," said Freddie. "With a reputation like yours, you don't need one. Let's have a round of applause for Candy, Carmella, and Limon!"

The audience complied.

Backstage, Gingerbread Beauty Boy hand's attended furiously to all the details. Mascara, floral spray blush, bark polish, whatever tiny detail it took to transform these trees into truly televised pageant queens, the Candywood makeover experts had it ready to use.

Frantic pageant fever grew. Shaking needles, clenched roots, and sappy nerves from all the contestants filled the dressing room.

Boosting the morale of the group was the always energetic, Candywood cream puff, celebrity Jose Éclair. Cleverly building the spirits of everyone, Jose recited a few lyrics from the opening number, lyrics meant everything to the crown-wearing hopefuls.

"If you want to be the best,
Put your fashion to the test,
Ordinary garland just won't do"

Bonk, Bonk, Bonk, Bonk. Bonk, Bonk, Bonk, Bonk. The driving dance beat of the orchestra vibrated throughout the entire building.

"Welcome to the first ever, televised Gingertown Christmas Eve Pageant. I am your host Freddie Molasses. Yes that's me on your televisions across the land. Are you ready? I said are you ready?" Freddie raised his arm high above his head and rotated it the same way a sports enthusiast would rally up fans as he ran off stage.

The crowd cheered.

The main curtain lifted. Flashing strobe lights, a rock candy mirror-ball, and a giant taffy-filled lava lamp shaped like a Christmas tree dominated the stage. Large globs of multicolored molten taffy bubbled and stretched into odd shapes inside the huge lamp. No one in this little town had ever seen anything like it.

Through cleverly cut holes on the main performance space, all twelve contestants rose up from under the stage in freeze-pose silhouetted positions, while singing choral harmonies to the opening song.

It's snowing
It's blowing

As winter winds start turning cold,
We know-oh……….
Our time has come to …..

(Bonk, bonk. Bonk, bonk, bonk!)

Pose

The stage lights flashed bright and suddenly the silhouetted contestants where now lit with an elegant frontal glow. Each tree changed to a new freeze statue position on the "Bonk, bonk. Bonk, bonk, bonk! Pose" music cue.

(Bonk, bonk. Bonk, bonk, bonk!)

Pose

(Bonk, bonk. Bonk, bonk, bonk!)

Pose

Ev'ry evergreen knows, knows.
You've got to strike your pose, pose. When it snows.
Ev'ry evergreen knows, knows.
You've got to strike your pose, pose. When it snows.

It was pure television magic. A spotlight highlighted the scrim. It parted in the middle. Out slid a small platform thrust with stairs in front of it, forward to center stage. On the thrust Freddie Molasses had repositioned himself to start the opening musical number. Screams from swooning audience members accented the visual excitement of this event to all the at home viewers as he began to sing.

Tis' the season to be fashioned
If this holiday's your passion
Time to shine, take center stage
With evergreens it's all the rage

Iza Miz-rooter, the celebrity fashion critic, could be heard announcing the trees as each paraded by the selected television camera and smiled. In typical pageant style, the contestants all sang in choral harmony with Freddie.

"Scotchie Forester"

"La Cona Pinesky"

"Shady Landers"

"Colorada Spruce"

"Debriss Firr"

"Twigla Yew"

"Branch Du Burr"

"Jodi Needles"

"Smokey Mosswood"

"Wintra Sapinbaum"

"Hope Evergreener and Cypress Limb"

Scotchie Forester

La Cona Pinesky

Shady Landers

Colorada Spruce

Debriss Firr

Branch Du Burr

Twigla Yew

Jodi Needles

Smokey Mosswood

Wintra Sapinbaum

Hope Evergreener

Cypress Limb

124

After the last tree was introduced the entire group lined up along the apron of the Barn theater stage to do their special half-whispered tongue twister pageant rap part of the song. Swinging shoulders, tapping toes, and bobbing heads filled the audience who were all rhythmically captivated.

Hemlock, Balsa, Douglas Firr
Cedar, White Pine, Juniper

Black Spruce, Blue Spruce, Irish Yew
Knotty Pine, you're super too!

Norfolk Pine, your limbs so fine
Scotch Pine, Red Pine, sweet as wine

Redwood Giant, Arborvitae
Evergreen so tall and mighty

Pose

An exhilarating percussion, base and instrumental solo took focus. The television crew out in the satellite tech van enhanced the program with modern creative editing for the home viewers. First they focused in on the spinning rock candy mirror ball, then to the live audience with the shimming patterns of reflected light, then to the bubble gum paparazzi's cameras all flashing eagerly at the onstage performers as the number continued.

The tech director counted down the seconds. "Five, four, three, two and ready for 'Talk to Camera', segment… go close up on Freddie."

Freddie Molasses poured it on. "Now that you've seen all of our twelve beautiful contestants this evening, let's hear what they have to say."

The first contestant spoke directly to the camera. "My name is La Cona Pinesky."

Redda Pinesky was in tears out in the audience, shouting loudly so all could hear. "That's my granddaughter! That's my little La Cona!"

"I am here to represent the glorious conifer population of South Carolina. My hobbies are collecting seashells, crossword puzzles, and planting baby carrots."

The red applause light glowed. La Cona walked down the long runway. As she did, Iza Miz-rooter described her attire for the camera. "Miss Pinesky is wearing a simple garment in free-flowing peach chiffon. The lilting chiffon train billows elegantly on the runway. A perfect choice."

"My name is Cypress Limb. I am originally from the northern hills of Kentucky. My hobbies are watching raindrops fall into a still pond, baking birthday cakes for cute little saplings, and playing hopscotch with foreign exchange students."

La Cona Pinesky
South Carolina
5' 10" - 115 lbs

Cypress Limb
Kentucky
5' 11" - 117 lbs

Jodi Needles
Gingertown
5'9" - 112 lbs

Iza Miz-rooter

Fashion
Reviewer

Iza added, "Miss Limb's introductory attire has a drop waist garment-line created by a sky-blue velvet sash. The sash coordinates beautifully with the tastefully executed powder-blue fabric body. How lovely!"

Cypress Limb winked at the judges once she reached the end of the runway. The audience was taken with her sweetness.

Next, approaching the camera as though it were her best friend, Jodi made a fantastic entrance. No longer the skinny tree with the gappy branches and thick glasses (thanks to new contact lenses), she was almost unrecognizable. The plain, natural beauty that everyone had come to take for granted had blossomed into another thing entirely. Her branches were each tipped with a lavender accent-spray. Jodi's opening outfit defied conventional pageant rules. She had on a bright tangerine-orange party dress with spaghetti straps.

"Hello everybody! My name is Jodi Needles, and I am your local Gingertown representative."

Everyone cheered.

"Eat sap, Redda!" Ida Mae was in the competitive spirit. "That's my beautiful Jodi, and she's a showstopper!" Sitting between Ida Mae and Great Aunt Sylvia, Grampa Joe cheered, holding his wife's hand in a shaking grip.

"My hobbies are teaching ladybugs to read, painting baby buggies with buttercup pollen, and providing a nursery school haven for hatching bluebirds in my upper limbs."

"Go in for a close-up," ordered the director in the control booth. "This is great for ratings!"

On the runway, Jodi gave a perfect smile to the judges as her attire was described by Iza as, "Fabulously daring!"

After Jodi made her entrance, Brian, who was sitting in the audience with the rest of the Needles Family, was getting antsy. He had lost his desire to see the remaining contestants introduce themselves during the first elimination round.

"Grampa, my roots are dry." And before anyone knew it, he was stomping up the main isle to get a drink. "Water fountain… Water fountain… Water fountain… Water fountain…" With only one thought on his mind, he continued to voice it out loud in a marching rhythm. "Water fountain... Water fountain... Water fountain... Water fountain... Water...?" Once in the lobby, the thought of a mere drink from the water fountain was usurped by a much sweeter desire.

Standing behind a large glass case filled with show snacks, a Cotton Candy Counter Lady spoke up. "Well hi there little shrub. What can I get for you?"

"I don't have any money."

"Oh don't worry Sweetie. After the show starts, no one cares what I do up here. Whatever you want - it's on the house. Go ahead, pick something! It'll be our little secret."

Brian liked this lady. She wasn't anything at all like the Topiaries, and he liked that she wasn't green, either. She was banana-yellow topped off with a hot-pink cotton-candy beehive. *I guess candy people are nicer to little trees than those snippy-clippy bushes were,* thought Brian. He had made up his mind. "I'll have a Sticky Sap Cola, ma'am."

"Ma'am schwa'am! If we're going to be friends, you'll have to call me Tee Zee Anne." She bent down to show Brian her nametag, which was pinned to her cotton-candy cashmere sweater. "And what's your name?"

"Brian."

"Well Brian, sweetie, what size would you like? We have the Itty Sippy, the Little Smacker, a plain old medium, the Large Tall-Long-Straw, or the Super Mega-Bucket Root-Soaker Deluxe!"

"I'll have the Super Mega-Bucket Root-Soaker Deluxe please, ma'am... I mean, Tee Zee Anne."

Ding, ding. The drink machine clanged when the drink dispenser button was pushed.

"Are you sure you can handle it?" grinned the counter lady.

"I'm sure. My sister Jodi is in the contest."

"That's nice."

"She's gonna win."

"That's real nice.," answered the counter lady as she continued to fill the gigantic drink container.

"'Cause she promised me that if she won, she'd..." Stopping in mid- sentence, Brian's train of thought came to a dead halt. He suddenly realized that he was standing right next to the rolling rack on which the two famous Gingertown percussion instruments were hanging.

"Do you know what those are?" said the Cotton Candy lady.

"I know what those are. That's the Grape Fizzy Soda-Stone Gong. It's made of polished grape fizzy soda-stone."

Ding, ding. The cup was now one quarter full.

"Why that's right."

The gong glistened like marbleized glass.

"And that's the perfectly pitched Golden Deep-Frozen Sorbet Triangle," marveled Brian.

"How does a little tree like you, know so much about these two instruments?"

"My Great Aunt Sylvia told me. She said the gong was dug up out of a big hole in Candyville - from the rock candy quarry - And they polished it, and they sanded it, and they made it almost in her back yard," explained Brian. "My Great Aunt Sylvia says she's lived there all her life."

"Candyville? I have cousins that live in Candyville," chimed Tee Zee Anne. "On my mother's side. The Mints. Spear and Pepper."

Ding, ding. The cup was now half full.

"I bet she knows my Uncle Chester. Between you and me, my uncle is as stale as an old Halloween treat, if you get my drift."

Brian giggled. "Wow." What his widening eyes fell upon now impressed him even more. Hanging next to the gong and the triangle were the Nut-Cluster Gong Mallet and the Golden Triangle-Wand.

Tee Zee Anne had more interesting tidbits about the two hanging candy percussion instruments. She talked on and on glibly as the cup continued to fill. Then suddenly she stopped mid-sentence. She had caught a glimpse of herself in the highly polished reflective surface of the gong. "Hmm, would you look at that!" she said, leaning forward to inspect her immense tangle of teased, sugary hair. "Looks like I need a touch up." As the finger of one hand continued to push the cola fill-lever, the other hand found its way to one of the white paper cone-shaped candy twirlers. Her bubbly blab never stopped as she twirled a fresh fluff of hot-pink spun-sugar cotton candy onto the white paper cone and applied it in huge swirling motions to the top of her head. When she had finished, the cone stuck out at the top of her pink hair at a crooked angle. "What do you think Sweetie?"

"It looks good enough to eat," smiled Brian.

"Where was I?" Then returning to her first thought, and still continuing to hold down the drink lever, Tee Zee Anne asked, "Did you know that once a year it takes four strong hard-taffy musclemen to carry that gong up to the top of the Gingertown fire station lookout tower?"

Ding, ding. The cup was now three-quarters full.

"How come?" Brian asked.

"It gets gonged up there to celebrate the first day of spring. And the Golden Deep-Frozen Sorbet Triangle is used every day at lunch time to start the Acapella Snow Singers in the town square all throughout the winter months."

"And I know what else they use 'em for too," said Brian. "Talent night!"

"If it's a tinga-linga…" said Tee Zee Anne.

"You're an in-ga," laughed Brian.

"And a gong-ger means?"

"You're a gon-ner."

Ding, ding, ding, ding. Ding, ding, ding, ding. Boink! "Here you go sweetie, all filled up," smiled Tee Zee Anne.

Brian reached up to grasp the enormous bucket-sized drink. It was so large, it had an airport luggage strap attached to it and small candy lifesaver wheels on the bottom.

"Excuse us, kid." Two oatmeal cookie stagehands draped a dark purple cover over the rack of instruments.

"Hurry up, Honey! You're gonna miss the show!" The counter lady winked at Brian. Brian sipped from the top of his cola and pulled the huge drink behind him towards the main aisle. But when no one was looking, he and his Super Mega-Bucket Root-Soaker Deluxe secretly slipped beneath the fabric cover and onto the cart.

The end of Chapter Ten

Chapter Eleven: A Sticky Situation

Sitting on the rack under the purple cloak, drinking his cola and taking licks off the Grape Fizzy Soda-Stone Gong, Brian was in bliss. Brian, like all young pranksters in Gingertown, knew that Sticky Sap Cola had another, ingenious use. In fact, most little Evergreener Gang trees knew this insider secret. They had discovered that, when mixed with different types of sweet candy treats, Sticky Sap Cola magically turned into Super Sticky Roof Glue. It was so sticky that all the town's people used it to hold the thousands of miniature cinnamon hearts that adorned the Gingertown rooftops in place.

Reaching up, Brian pulled down both the Nut-Cluster Gong Mallet and the Golden Triangle-Wand. Then the mischievous little tree dipped each into the Sticky Sap Cola. He stirred them round and round, watching his drink melt away the candy handles. Then he lifted each one out in order to taste his super-sticky sweet concoction.

"Nope, not done yet."

Then he dipped and swirled them again, creating more sugary film on the top of the cola drink. When his potion had just the right color and flavor, the cart suddenly began to move.

"These instruments seem heavier than usual today," said one of the oatmeal cookie stagehands.

Brian snickered as they rolled him and the rack to a new location. With the large drink bucket positioned between his knees, Brian watched the cola as it sloshed back and forth. Then the cart came to an abrupt, bumping stop, and Sticky Sap Cola splashed upward covering the gong and the triangle in thick syrupy goo. It was now dripping off both instruments. Luckily, he didn't get any on himself. Peeking out from under the fabric, Brian could see the backs of the seats on which the celebrity judges sat. He giggled to himself, for he had an instinctive knack for mischief, and he could guess what would happen next.

"And there you have it! Our top twelve competing evergreen trees!" chimed in Freddie. "But as we all know, it's now time for the judges to narrow our twelve treelightful lovelies down to the final four. Who do you think will continue on this evening to compete for the title of Miss Gingertown? And which treemendous treetop will end up this evening's Top Tree? Let's ask, shall we?" Freddie Molasses turned to the judges.

At that very moment, the cloak was yanked off the rack. No one took notice of the Needles family's youngest member, as everyone was focused on what the Master of Ceremonies was saying to the camera. Brian saw his chance and quickly scooted beneath the judges' table, hiding under the table-cloth.

"Just look at all the graceful green that we have up here tonight." Freddie's charming demeanor sent shivers through the onstage trees. "As I read your name, please step forward to receive your critique. Scotchie Forester."

A spotlight glowed brighter as Miss Forester stepped forward. She was the first of the trees, who were now all standing proudly in one long row across the length of the stage from left to right. Limon spoke first. "I thought this was an evergreen beauty pageant, not a scrub brush look-a-like contest." Boos and laughter rolled through the crowd.

Carmella was next. "I love each and every one of you," she beamed, forcing an all-too-big-of-a-smile at the camera. Carmella then fluttered her coconut sparkle eyelashes. The audience cheered.

Candy Jawbreaker sat for a silent micro-second. Then he tilted his deep burgundy gumball head in a hip candy way, holding his white sugar disk hat on his head and spoke to the crowd. "I have to agree with Limon on this one. Scotchie, you just don't do the holiday zing-thing for me." Reaching forward, the hip, candy-cluster judge with the gumball head pointed his finger to push a button on the table. The sound of a giant flush rattled through the theater and out to a million televisions coast-to-coast. A wave of bawdy laugher soon followed the tasteless sound effect.

With that, Limon happily reached behind his seat for the Nut-Cluster Gong Mallet, which was still in the super-sized mega cola bucket. He quickly grabbed hold of the handle, lifting it up and out of Brian's drippy liquid masterpiece. The oozy feel of the grip had not slowed down the momentum of Limon's joyous anticipation of gonging his first victim that night. With a fueled up, full forced shouldering arm swing, Limon whacked the gong with all his might.

B-Wong-ang-ang-ang-ang!

A giant red-and-white-striped candy hook appeared from the wings and instantly yanked Scotchie Forester off the stage.

Mr. Limon Sour's sardonic grin was suddenly replaced by a look of puzzlement. The mallet-wielding judge realized that his grip was stuck to the stick, which was in turn sappy-cola glued to the center of the marbleized disk.

Proceeding with the live broadcast, Freddie read from the next cue card. "La Cona Pinesky, step forward please."

Redda, who was sitting up in the balcony, had brought a basket of confetti. She tossed colorful party bits up in the air and over the balcony railing in joyous glee for her granddaughter. The bulk of it landed right on Limon, covering his increasingly sticky mess with multi-colored grit.

Still standing, Limon Sour continued, however unsuccessfully, to attempt to un-stick himself. "If I had a free hand, I would gong the whole lot of them. But Miss Pinesky seems to be in luck, as I do not… seem… to… have… the… strength… to…" Limon gritted his sour gummy lips while pulling on the messy mallet, which was now hopelessly stuck to his hand. "Mmmm!"

"Coming from you, I think we'll take that as a positive review," commented Freddie, as he stood next to La Cona, oozing with charm.

"Yea!" Redda tossed more confetti.

The sweetest of the three judges, Carmella, changed her pose. Now smiling into another camera, with her hands placed coyly just below her pink candy-heart chin, she spoke. "I love each and every one of you." The crowd cheered again.

"Well if my limey friend here doesn't have the strength to gong Miss Pinesky," interjected judge Jawbreaker, "I must then choose to give her a "Tinga-linga."

The chubby jawbreaker judge reached for the golden stick. It too was still in the bucket of cola goo. With the delicate wave of a fairy wand, Candy Jawbreaker drew a pretty, pinging ting from the hanging triangle.

A crown of roses dropped from above and onto La Cona's treetop head.

But when the jovial judge pulled the wand away from the three-sided instrument, he created thick, gooey cola-web strands. The harder he tried to pull the sugary glue-strings off, the more they spread. Frantically attempting to de-web himself, he accidentally got the ever-stretching web tangled up in Carmella's tutti-frutti hairstyle.

"Ah!" She squeaked a peeping scream as her gloriously manicured candy fingertips were now also stuck to her hair. She pulled. "Oww!" She pulled again. "Owwww!!! How is it that whenever I go anywhere with the two of you, I end up a sticky mess?" Miss Cashew, always the professional, forced yet another smile toward the nearest camera.

Limon, still pulling with all of his might, lifted one of his citrus-shoed feet up to the gong for better leverage. As the mallet pulled away from the center of the gong, the bungee-corded, springy elastic sap was stretched as far as Limon's arm could reach. Then as fast as he pulled it away, the opposing energy of the elastic goo yanked his arm back. Bong! He pulled again. *Bong! And again, Bong!* And then with many fast rapid bouncing pulls, *Bong, bong, bong, bong!* But still he was unable to break free.

Freddie laughed, as did the audience. "I think you only get one gong per tree, Limon. Ha ha ha ha ha! And I haven't even gotten to introduce the next contestant." The audience laughed.

For no other reason than pure reflex, Carmella, now in the middle of the goo entanglement, smiled a chicklety grin. "I love each and every one of you." The audience cheered once again. "We love you, too, Carmella!" shouted an anonymous fan.

Looking down at the Super Mega-Bucket Root-Soaker Deluxe, the angry lemon-lime judge realized his dilemma. "I think I've been Sticky Sap Cola stuck!"

"Ooo, it's getting on my new shoes! Icky! Icky!" Carmella was losing her camera composure as the sappy mess continued to spread.

"They don't call me 'The Jawbreaker' for nothin'!" declared Candy Jawbreaker. He puffed and puffed like a power weightlifter psyching himself out for the big lift, then pulled frantically, attempting to untangle himself one more time.

Ta-ding, Bong, Ling-ga, Wang-ang-ang-ang. Thwack! The instrument rack, the sticky instruments, and the three judges all fell over in a comical crash.

The crowd roared at what looked like planned antics.

"A laugh riot!"

"They are so funny!"

"No wonder they're so popular!"

Lying at the bottom of the jumbled mess with his head to one side, Limon Sour was now nose-to-nose with Brian, his own head poking out from under the bottom of the judges' table, laughing. "Why you little…" But before Limon could move, Brian scooted away under the draped runway that thrust out from the apron of the stage, and made his way underneath, bolting through the orchestra pit, upsetting several music stands that lay in his path.

Freddie stepped forward, microphone in hand. "Let's have a big round of Ginger-town applause for tonight's comic celebrity judges. If I didn't know better, I'd confuse the three of you for the Three Sponge-Candy Stooges." Once again, everyone roared with laughter. "Only on live television, folks."

"Not on *my* live television!" Seeing the antics of the judges from her backstage perspective, Ms. Hemlock was not at all pleased. "I just knew those Candywood celebrity sugar-substitute judges could never be trusted. This is a dignified beauty pageant. *My* dignified beauty pageant. Not some slap-sticky stic-com with a sappy laugh track."

"But everyone thought it was really funny!" Little Ronnie Barkwood pulled back the stage curtain to reveal that even the musicians were laughing.

Canadia's evening-gloved hands turned into knotted fists of frustration. "Not while I'm in charge!"

Little Ronnie saw yet another opportunity and seized it. "Well, I think that, in the best interest of the pageant, the first thing we have to do is fire the emcee. Now that the crowd is all warmed up, I can tell jokes while you take over for the judges. It'll be just like we planned it. That is… before all those sweet-talking cookie-cutter television execs took over."

"No Ronald, I will handle this mutiny my way." Canadia stamped off towards a large canvas travel case. Clearly printed across it were the words, "The Drama Bag." She reached into the bag and pulled out a huge pair of scissors. Waving them in the air she declared, "We are going to nip this swamp-weed behavior in the bud. Here Ronald. You know what to do."

"Me? Why me? I should be telling jokes." She handed him the oversized shiny silver shears. "Do you remember the milkweed and tree tar incident? From the Rolling Hills Texicana Pine Pageant? Hmmm?"

Reluctantly, Ronnie answered. "Yes ma'am."

"And how you looked like an oversized dandelion poof while having to ride all the way home on the bus, which was full of snide-remark-slinging lumber-stud rootball players! Remember all that I had to do to get the pod-fuzzies off of your needles? Hmm?"

"Yes ma'am."

Taking orders like a soldier, little Ronnie saluted the pageant general. "My mission awaits." He marched out, scissors in hand. Under his breath, he was saying to himself, "I'm funnier than all of them put together."

Ronnie Barkwood approached the sappy-stuck judges holding the huge scissors. "I hate doing this, but it must be done."

A horror of hesitation filled the crowd as little Ronnie Barkwood lifted his scissors toward Limon. "Pull!" he shouted. "Pull your arm. Hard!"

As Limon stretched the elastic glue-strand, Ronnie reached forward to snip it off him. The stand broke loose splattering onto Ronnie's impeccably shined Oxford root boots like a big sugar booger-snot. "Yuck." Ronnie looked as though he were suddenly ill.

Doing his duty, Canadia's loyal treesistant continued to unstick the trio. But in his haste, he accidentally snipped off Carmella's sugared orange-slice of a ponytail. Before she could notice, Candy, Limon and Ronnie quickly worked together to reattach it to her head with a gob of cola glue.

As this front row activity was underway, Canadia bee-lined it directly to the Master of Ceremonies, Freddie Molasses.

As she approached, her scary, angry expression was reserved for Freddie and Freddie alone. In one clean yank, she snatched the wireless microphone out of his hand and in the next instant she turned to face the audience with a perfect pageant smile.

"Hello everybody. I am Canadia Hemlock or, as the loving citizens of Gingertown have come to know me, the Pageant Lady."

Addressing the live audience, Ms. Hemlock was able to communicate her distaste with subtle sarcasm.

"Let's have big thumbs-up for the foolish, childish, infantile-ish, almost insect biting-ish, stinging humor of our judges. But according to the pageant rules, and I quote,

'In the event of a mishap where the judges are deemed unfit to uphold their sacred obligations due to illness, insanity, incarceration,' - and I have now added idiot-cola-glue-disorder to the list! - 'The pageant director,' - that would be me - 'has the authority to step in' and last, but not least, my decisions are final!"

Then, moving abruptly across the stage, the Pageant Lady finished the first elimination round, pointing at and man-handling the trees in a manner accurately reflecting her current state of mind.

"You're in! You're out! Definitely out. In. Out. Didn't-pay-her-pageant-dues-on-time-dear out. In. Out. Out. And very, very, pack-your-bags-out!"

Upon Canadia's declaration of who would remain, the newly disqualified trees were yanked off the stage with more giant red-and-white-striped hooks. The remaining girls were instantly adorned with flower crowns. Ida Mae shook with pride, as Jodi had been chosen to be one of the four finalists. Redda was shouting at the top of her lungs, all the while spewing great heaping wads of confetti on those in the audience below.

The end of Chapter Eleven

Chapter Twelve: Talent Trouble

The first elimination round had the home viewers completely hooked. This was going to be a great show.

"And let's give it up for our remaining lovely green things - Ms. Cypress Limb, Ms. La Cona Pinesky, Ms. Debriss Firr, and Ms. Jodi Needles!" Freddie Molasses held his grin until the little red light on the camera went out.

Running backstage during the commercial break, Jodi's sweet-as-pie television face was back to her normal-skeptical-Jodi-face. When she reached her changing area, Julie was standing there waiting to assist with the change.

"Argh, get these disgusting little crap machines out of my hair." Jodi shook the bluebirds out of her branches and onto the makeup table.

Julie was as happy as if she herself were in the pageant. "It worked. They love you."

The television director had just received a newsflash. "Go to the park," he instructed his crew, switching to the live onsite reporter for a breaking story.

"We interrupt this broadcast to bring to you, live, the outside mayhem. It appears that a protest rally has started in this quaint little cookie village. The Junior Leafers, surrounded by supporters, are standing in front of the Sequoia Red Fountain, with the blinking neon lights from the Barn right behind them. The Leafers are holding an array of protest signs."

Crabby Apples addressed the camera first. "My name is Crabby Apples, and I am here on behalf of forest trees everywhere."

Elma Wood pushed into the camera shot. "Leaf exfoliation is nothing to be ashamed of."

"There is more to winter beauty than glass balls and popcorn necklaces!" added Silvera Birch.

"Why have you chosen to protest in front of this statue?" inquired the reporter.

"Treequality! And where better to make our cause known than here, in front of the Sequoia Red Fountain. We, the Junior Leaf, are making a stand on behalf of all leaf growing trees. Deciduous trees have just as much of a right to be a part of this annual event as any ordinary needled specimen. And the fact that we do exfoliate for the winter months only adds to our unique beauty. After all, have you ever met a pine tree with cheek bones like these?" stated Wanda Walnut with pride.

The surrounding crowd of Junior Leafers snickered in support.

"The Junior Leaf intends to grow in numbers and supplant and replant Gingertown's outdated prejudice with a more modern point of view," concluded Wanda Walnut.

And as always, Oakanna Acorn had the final word, "Beauty is only bark deep!"

"You heard it here first. This is Graham Jelly Roll reporting live from Gingertown. And now, back to the pageant."

The home viewing audience didn't miss much. The talent portion had already begun. Standing on stage in front of a painted backdrop of a Kentucky farm, Cypress Limb was dressed in her country clogger best. She had on a high teased, dark brown needle wig, with a little blue bow in it. Her outfit was a white and blue gingham-printed dress with a ruffled pink crinoline underneath. Her two skinny trunk legs were exposed from the knees down. She was wearing white tights and shiny black rubbery shoes. During the intro, while standing there waiting for her chance to start singing, the twang of the country guitars put her into a hip-swinging motion.

I was just a wee thing, a cute little hillbilly seedling
Dandelions an' thistles were my friends
Doing chores and cleaning up messes
Swamp flies stuck to my spider web dresses
Havin' daylight dreams of places far away

Cypress Limb sang her heart out. So much so that all of the backstage helpers and waiting contestants gathered in the wings to listen.

Now that I'm older
Standin' as tall as an elephant's shoulder
I help my momma and my papa work the farm

Julie, mixed in with the onlookers, noticed her little brother in the group. "Brian! What are you doing back here?"

Brian stuck out his tongue at her and ran away. Fearing the worst, Julie chased after him.

Cypress Limb slowly moved downstage in order to sing a little closer to the judges.

> I come from poor country bumpkins
> Rooted in a patch of trailer-park pumpkins
> Hoping for my chance to break away.

The painted canvas scrim of Kentucky was beginning to wave slightly in the front. As Cypress Limb sang, the audience could see the silhouette of Brian and Julie fighting just behind it. Everyone confused it for part of the act.

"Come back here you little brat! Why are you back here?"

"You're here," yelled Brian.

"I'm helping. And you promised to behave, remember? We had a deal!"

"I'm helping too." Brian continued to play cat and mouse with Julie behind the scrim. Strangely, each line that Cypress Limb sang seemed comically coordinated with the children's shadowed movements.

> I asked my papa,
> "Will there be daylight dreams for me?"
>
> He said, "Cypress Limb,
> You quit nagging me, girl, an' go ask your ma."
>
> So I asked my momma,
> "Will there be daylight dreams for me?"
> And this is what she sweetly sang to me.

Julie had chased Brian out from behind the scrim. Without knowing it, they both added a flair of unexpected comedy to the Cypress' act.

"You should be out front with Gramma and Grampa," Julie whispered in a loud stage-whispery way.

Brian teasingly mimicked her whispering. "I'm getting water!" and off he ran. Just above the drinking fountain, a black and white backstage monitor was illuminated. Brian watched Cypress Limb finish her song.

> Reach for the sun
> You'll be number one
> Raise your branches high above the rest

Brian got up on a step to get a drink. He licked the spout instead.

The at-home viewers were entranced by Cypress. On color television, she was even more radiant than in person.

> You must keep on believin'
> That a poor Kentucky Seedlin'
> Can grow up to be a country Christmas star!

"She was great," Jodi muttered to herself. But Jodi also knew that she couldn't let herself be psyched out. "Focus, focus. Believe it, see it, believe it, see it. Where have you been?" Jodi was about to scream with frustration. "I'm on in two seconds and you're doing shadow puppets. Well, it didn't help. You just made her act funnier."

"What are you talking about?" Julie had no idea of what she had just done.

"Never mind. Help me get this out," ordered Jodi.

Together they rolled out a big prop-box, Jodi pulling from the front, Julie pushing from behind. The box, on low smooth casters, was as tall as a washing machine. Each side was painted a different solid color.

Julie quietly backed herself offstage. Gramma gave her a quick little wave from the audience.

Lightly humming, finger snapping, soft-shoe music began. Jodi stood center in a glamorous spotlight. She had on a full-length red satin cape with a tall red satin top hat to match. Jodi could see the entire audience staring at her. Hundreds of fans, school friends, neighbors, strangers, and celebrities were all waiting for her to best the previous act. *Stop thinking!* A whispery little inner voice told her. *Focus on the little red light.* That was the advice Ms. Hemlock had given her. "Pretend it's just you and the little red light, alone in your bedroom playing pageant queen games."

The music vamped again waiting for Jodi to begin. Redda whispered to her friends, "Just like Ida and on television too!"

"Light… my room… light… my room…" Jodi spoke to herself, getting into a calm rhythm. She started singing softly…

Just when there's nothing left to ooh about… **poof!**

Jodi threw up her arms. A shower of rainbow glitter twinkled to the floor. Magic flowers popped out from under her sleeves. She tossed them to the judges.

There's a surprise

The audience applauded.

Just when there's **nothing left** to ahh about... whoosh!

Again she made a large graceful arch with her arms. This time
bubbles came out of nowhere to fill the stage.

Here's a surprise...

Gramma and Grampa shook with pride.

Just **when** you think you've **seen** all you can see,
Just when **your** day **is** really, really passé,
Just when there's **nothing** left up your sleeve... Voila!

Jodi flipped her dark red cape off.

There's a surprise!

Underneath, was a crazy colorful outfit made from every possible scrap of fabric and trinket that Julie and Gramma could find. The audience laughed.

> Life is full of surprises,
> small compromises.
> It has disguises that lead us on our way.

The outer layer of the colorful dress dropped to the stage, revealing an even brighter, tighter fitting dress under it. Again the audience applauded. Jodi opened one side of the huge multicolored box to show that the interior was empty.

> Some people look in an empty box and say,
> "Hey, there's nothing inside!"
>
> And some people take all the money they've earned.
> "This $22 .83 is from helping my neighbors plant
> flower pot ferns."

Jodi removed her hat to take out her hidden money.

> Then toss it in a sock, stash it in a box,
> covered up in locks, and save it for a rainy day.

Jodi tossed the money into a hole in the top of the box. Then she quickly put all the locks on the front door of the box. A watering can was unveiled. She sprinkled water into the hole.

> "Here comes the rain."
> So it'll grow, when it's cold, into gold,
> when I'm old, so I'm told.

"To my magical recipe I add three fresh chicken eggs."

"Next two ordinary pet hamsters named Dino and Frank."

"With their wiggly green noses, toe-es and legs."

"Compliments of my little sister who now I'd like to thank."

From within one of the many colorful fabric-patch pockets sewn onto her costume, Jodi pulled out the two little guys. She then dropped both hamsters into the box. What was going to happen next had everybody in the theater on the edge of their seats. She continued to sing as she rotated the large colorful box for all to see.

Life has twists and turns, that can spin us about,
it goes around and around and around.
Life has so many magical surprises, compromises and disguises.
So don't... try to figure it out!

The box stopped rotating. Taking her wand, Jodi tapped on the four locks. In turn, each fell off. The door fell open. Out came Tiger Lily balancing on a large circus ball like a trained poodle. The unhappy cat was wearing a little yellow rain coat and a rubber hat with booties to match. Covered in eggs and water, Tiger Lily could only groan a mad cat groan, as her mouth was quite full at that moment. In her bite she held a small basket, and in that basket Dino and Frank wiggled their little noses at the audience.

Life is full of surprises, so don't try to figure it out.

Blackout.

The audience was thrilled with her act.

"Take *that*, Miss Red Garland and Silver Stars!" Ida Mae was over-joyed for Jodi.

Tiger Lily tippy-toed the ball into the wings. Julie was standing there in the dark waiting to retrieve her pets. Tiger Lily jumped into Julie's arms. Upon doing so, Dino and Frank fell out of the basket.

"Oh no!" Julie tossed Tiger Lily to Jodi and ran after them. "Dino! Frank!"

Redda held the printed program, pointing out her name as a former winner. She shushed everyone around her. "My granddaughter is on next. Shh."

Dramatic opening music swelled to a loud climax. Looking down from her balcony seat, Redda had her camera ready to catch La Cona's grand entrance.

Gracefully running across the stage, La Cona appeared to be float-ing on her pointe shoes. Deciding not to be just another forgettable singer, she had chosen to do ballet. The lower branches of La Cona's figure had been lifted high up into a flat French tutu, and all of her head-branches had been pulled back into a tight needle-bun. She moved about the stage with great seriousness. The panel of judges was impressed with her technique.

While La Cona performed, Jodi was busy at her dressing table, struggling to get out of her magic costume. "Where have you been? You're supposed to be helping me change. Stop running around."

Julie's little green face had a sad expression. "I can't find Dino and Frank. They fell out of the basket."

"Don't worry about it now," Jodi said. "I'll get you all the hamsters you want after the contest."

Huddled into a tight corner under the water fountain, Dino and Frank were retrieved by the mysterious white-gloved individual. This was the same gloved one responsible for the banner cable snapping, as well as the loose bolts on the big lime-green "G." Step by step, holding tight to the scared little pets, the secret naysayer climbed to the top of the catwalk above the stage. No one noticed. Looking down on La Cona, a plan to ruin her performance was next on the list.

"Serious? Ridiculous would be the correct adjective," whispered this pageant villain.

The white-gloved individual watched closely the timing of her movements, and just as she slowed to a grounded pose, the two little hamsters were dropped into the Ballerina's headdress. So small were the hamsters, and so fast was this prank, that not even the TV crew caught it.

La Cona took long, elegant strides. She reached and stretched. Confident that she was winning over the judges, she smiled to them all.

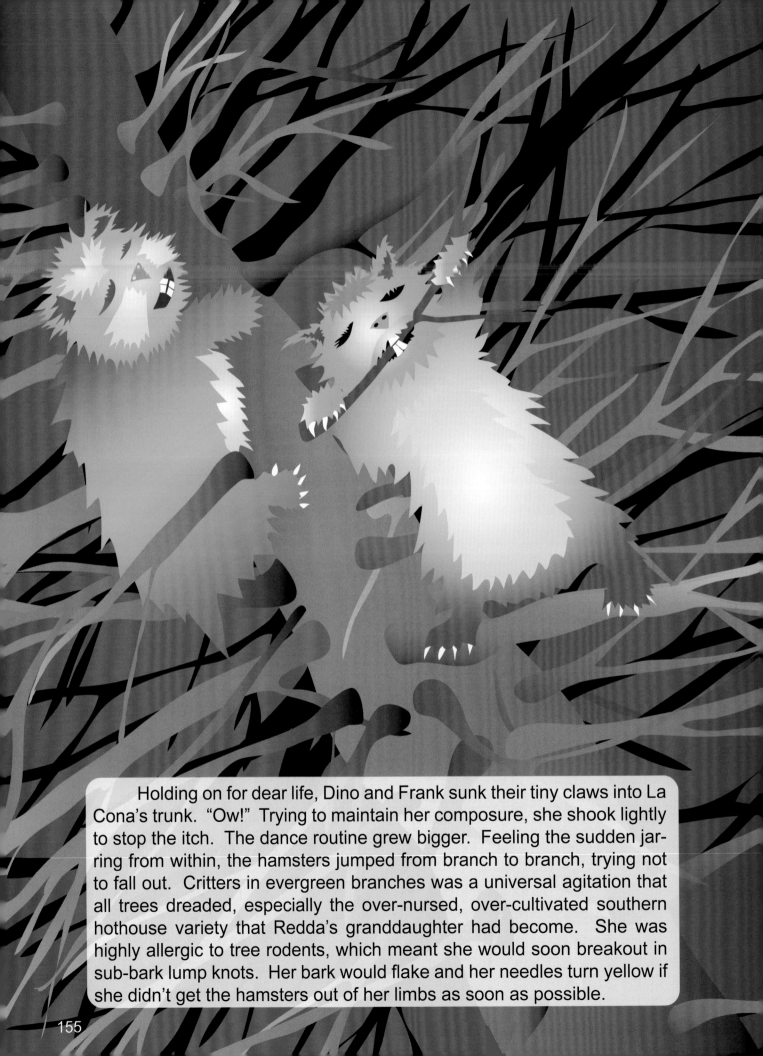

Holding on for dear life, Dino and Frank sunk their tiny claws into La Cona's trunk. "Ow!" Trying to maintain her composure, she shook lightly to stop the itch. The dance routine grew bigger. Feeling the sudden jarring from within, the hamsters jumped from branch to branch, trying not to fall out. Critters in evergreen branches was a universal agitation that all trees dreaded, especially the over-nursed, over-cultivated southern hothouse variety that Redda's granddaughter had become. She was highly allergic to tree rodents, which meant she would soon breakout in sub-bark lump knots. Her bark would flake and her needles turn yellow if she didn't get the hamsters out of her limbs as soon as possible.

Meanwhile, the two unwelcome guests held on tighter and tighter. Higher and higher she jumped. The steps that she had practiced evolved into an abstract, avant-garde dance routine. The audience, thinking this was just a variation on the classics, laughed.

"This green thing has got it goin' on!" commented Freddie to the audience. Everyone laughed even harder.

Completely surprised by her granddaughter's act, Redda quickly tried to explain to her friends. "A comic ballerina genius! Who knew?"

The number was coming to an end. No longer fearing a possible fall and a trampling, Dino and Frank stopped their clawing and biting. During her bow, the two little hamsters jumped off and scurried off the stage right to Julie. She put them in their travel cage. La Cona saw this in her peripheral vision. She smiled politely to all, but this was not over. Not by a long shot!

"You!!" Shaking with anger, La Cona was burning mad.

Before La Cona could move any closer, Jodi stepped in front of her sister. "Yes?"

Cypress Limb stood at La Cona's side, for added support.

"I am highly allergic to rat bites, woodchuck chews, and critter nests," accused La Cona.

"My hamsters are not rats!" Julie shouted.

"Close enough!" Cypress Limb added.

Before a screaming match got rolling, Ms. Hemlock intervened. "Rule number three hundred forty-seven, page seventy-nine, paragraph two: 'Lady Green conduct must always be followed.' No matter how much you hate your competitor, you must always do it with a smile. After the pageant, you can pull each other's needles out. But now we have a show to put on. Gettit? Gottit? Good! Go! Bye, bye."

Of course, Brian now popped up right in the middle of everyone, adding yet another level of tension with a goofy smile.

"Augh! I'm going to feed you to the wood chipper when this is done." La Cona turned to her dressing area with the slight twitch of beginning allergies. Angry squint-eyed glances were shared by all.

"Girls, girls, girls. We only have 96 seconds." Jose Éclair and his gingerbread beauty makeover boys swarmed the dressing room. "Don't be shy. There is nothing that we haven't seen. Boy trees, girl trees, during a pageant we are all just trees. Spray, clippers, hot glue guns, hurry, hurry, hurry!"

In a matter of seconds, each of the four finalists had a crew of gingerbread beauty boys assigned to them. Tucking, painting, even wood sanding. Whatever it took to prepare the girls for the next leg of the pageant, they did it. The remaining contestants, who were also a part of the fashion parade segment, had to complete their own beauty makeovers. In the midst of the confusion, the mysterious gloved hand was at it again.

Little things that never seem terribly important actually are, when you are participating in a pageant - things like an acceptance speech, a special necklace given for good luck, a bright fuchsia ostrich feather, or perhaps a box of ornaments. The gloved villain took them all without arousing suspicion.

"Where are my pantyhose?"

"Who took my shoes?"

"How did my lights get tangled up?"

"Not to worry ladies, for I have an enormous sack of trim balls and beauty products. Help yourselves." Jose Éclair was trampled nearly flat by the girls as they all looked for replacements. The gloved troublemaker had failed this time.

"Welcome back to Gingertown's Christmas Eve Pageant. I am still your host, yes that's me on your televisions across the land. Here they are! Pretty green things… in evening wear!"

The crowd cheered.

The main curtain lifted. A parade of sashaying trees included all the contestants, even the ones that had been eliminated in the first round.

Down the runway they went. A pageant choral number set the pace as Freddie serenaded the girls.

> Jing jing, ting a ling, ting ting, bing bing.
> Jing jing, ting a ling, ting ting, bing bing.
>
> The Prettiest Tree in Gingertown
> Will wear a magic golden crown!
>
> Strolling down the runway with the scepter in her hand.
>
> She's so slap happy, she could do the Fox Trot,
> Charleston, Varsity Drag!

All the trees now had curvaceous feminine figures. Gone were the silhouettes of the tired old Christmas trees. Tucked and jammed into underlining corsets, all of their branches had been rearranged to accommodate evening gowns.

"Why can't they clip themselves like that all the time?" said Father Topiary. He and his two daughters were particularly fond of this part.

> Jing jing, ting a ling, ting ting, bing bing.
> Jing jing, ting a ling, ting ting, bing bing.
> She is the Ooo, Ahhh, Prettiest Tree,
>
> She is the "Oh, My!" New Tree with a zing.
> Her smile so sappy, lips like taffy,
> The cute-est little Christmas thing.

The viewing audience heard Iza Miz-rooter's voice as the cameras followed the fashion divas. "Each girl is allowed to show her own style and vision of what a Christmas Eve tree should look like."

> The Prettiest Tree in Gingertown,
> Will wear a magic golden crown.

Everyone applauded as each tree took center stage. Green on green, blue back-less, layered white lace; each one was more extraordinary than the last. The crowd's already high energy level lifted even higher as the four finalists made their entrances.

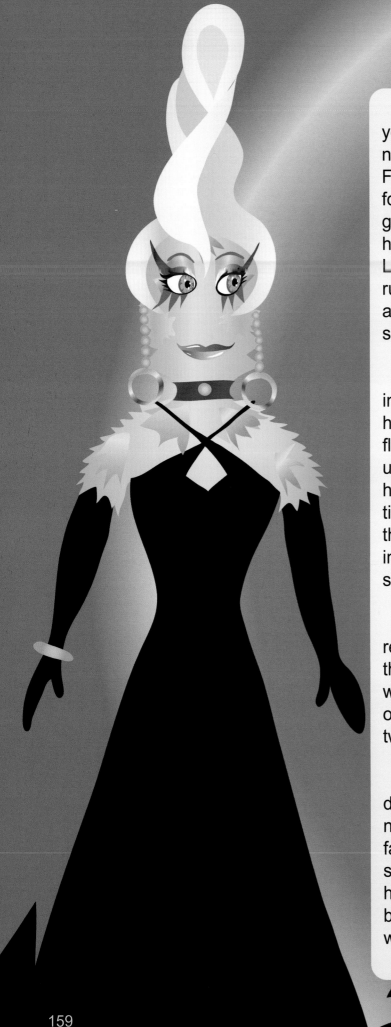

"And now here they come, the trees you've been waiting for, this evening's finalists. First we have Debriss Firr from Florida, wearing a pineapple gold sequined form-fitting dress. That must be hard to get into," Iza laughed. "And now, making her party strut down the runway, Cypress Limb! Oh, how lovely in a layered off-white ruffled classic. An elegant choice. Look at the lovely train and the long billowing sleeves."

With only two left to go, Jodi stood in position. Wrapped in a cloak to keep her gown a surprise, at the last second it flew to the ground. The crowd was swept up in immediate controversy. Though Jodi had initially balked at the idea, she had ultimately decided to wear black. People in the audience murmured responses ranging from "I love it!" to "I hate it!" to quite simply "Oh my!"

"I don't know what to say, exactly," reported Iza Miz-rooter. "It would appear that Miss Jodi Needles is determined to win this race. Black. Shocking. Unheard of. But also gorgeous! This reviewer gives two roots up."

Jodi was a vision of innovative holiday spirit. She wore a full upswept blond needled wig, just a hint of golden-green face spray accented by purple lips and eye shadow. "I am going to win this," she told herself as she strutted, swinging her hips back and forth to the very end of the runway.

Having returned to their front row positions, the three celebrity judges had been reinstated by Canadia after being completely de-stuck from the Sticky Sap Cola mess. Carmella Cashew and Candy Jawbreaker stood up to applaud Jodi. The black sleeveless dress shocked and titillated everyone. Limon Sour gave Jodi a sour wink of approval.

Not to be outdone by her competition, La Cona was last and had only seconds to outdo Jodi. In a rage of competitive spirit, she ripped the front of her red gown into a deep plunging neckline. She quickly pulled open the front of her corset to reveal as much green needle-cleavage as she could. "If they want spectacle, then that's what I'll give them," she told herself.

"And our final contestant, the always tasteful Miss La Cona… Pinesky?! Oh, Freddie!" commented Iza on camera, "We have yet another new trendsetter here for holiday tree fashions."

"Sexy and green, that's how I like my Christmas trees," laughed Freddie.

Redda had nothing to say. Her granddaughter was stealing the show, but at what cost? Whoever heard of a sexy Christmas Eve tree? she thought. Even Limon Sour was impressed with La Cona's gown.

La Cona, who had now taken her place on the stage with the rest of the contestants, directed a sly glance of intended victory right at Jodi.

"And there you have it, all of our holiday beauties and the four stunning Top Tree finalists," said Freddie as he gestured toward the contestant-filled stage while still smiling into the camera.

Once out of camera shot, the other contestants' cute "hellos" and false-ringing "Let's be friends after the pageant!" turned into a veritable tempest of jealous nitpicking. "They should both be disqualified!"

"On what grounds?" Ms. Hemlock found nothing wrong. "They both followed the rules and took their visions to a new height. If you want to win you must be rootless." She knew all too well.

The end of Chapter Twelve

Chapter Thirteen: Winning

Before anyone had time to stop clamoring over the parade of lovely gowns, the music changed to another driving dance beat. Blue lights flooded the stage. Watery reflections spilled out into the theater and onto the live audience. A gigantic sponge-candy starfish and rubbery squid were lowered as a backdrop. The tentacles moved by remote control located high up in the tech booth.

Julie stood next to Jodi backstage, waiting. "Jodi, you're going to win. I can feel it. See? I told you black would shake them all up."

"Yes, you were right little sister, I admit it. What's with the crazy outfit?"

Julie had transformed herself with a mix-and-match variety of decorations found in Jose Éclair's big bag of trims.

"I want to be ready to greet our public when we win," explained Julie.

"Do you have my swim balls?"

"They're right here." Julie opened the box of ornaments. "These aren't them."

"What do you mean? I have to wear swim balls for this segment. It's in the rule-book, remember? 'Balance and poise doth a pageant lady create.'" Peering into the box, Jodi gasped, "Are you crazy? I can't wear these. How?"

The swim balls that Julie and Gramma had so meticulously painted had been switched. Their imaginative idea had been to paint each little glass orb with a fish, and then glitter them so they would look real on stage. Well, what they had planned had been given a new twist. Every ball in the box was filled with water, and inside each orb was a real live fish, just like the ones Brian had in his fish tank. Both sisters' immediate reaction was to blame Brian, but even he didn't have the wherewithal to plan such a prank… or did he?

"Just put them on me and I'll make do somehow."

"All fifty of them?" said Julie in shock.

"Yes all fifty," ordered Jodi. "And hurry up!"

Another of Canadia's pageant rules stated that each girl had to carry 50 swim trim-balls. To quote Ms. Hemlock: "This is the only way to prove a contestant's poise and fitness." However, water-filled globes had never, ever been mentioned as a requirement.

"Having a little problem?" La Cona smiled with evil delight.

"No. I am doing just fine." Standing with close to fifty extra pounds of water and live fish inside the swim trim ornaments, Jodi took a deep breath.

"Think teacups and tennis shoes," said Julie.

Waiting on her mark, Jodi had to walk down the runway, stand on the X, turn, pose for photographers, and walk back to her assigned spot. How hard could it be? The little fish inside the balls all looked out at the bright lights. They all began swimming in fast circles, which didn't help Jodi's balance at all. "Cut it out!" she said under her breath. In unison, little fish all stopped and stared at Jodi.

"Here she comes, Miss Jodi Needles," commented Iza Miz-rooter.

While onstage, Jodi could hear the announcer's voice emanating from the backstage monitors. "She's wearing nothing but glass orbs, cleverly arranged in the pattern of a two piece bikini bathing suit. Her head is wrapped in a terrycloth turban, and open rooted high-heeled sandals adorn her woody feet."

"How did I get myself into this?" Jodi muttered under her breath. "Look at all these people staring at me. To them, I'm just another piece of wood. Stop it, Jodi! Focus. Focus!" Jodi looked at the cameramen, the flashing lights - it was all so overwhelming that she felt herself trembling under the weight of the heavy fish balls which were almost too much for her skinny frame to handle. Strength, she thought. Teacup strength. Ten troublesome turquoise… Jodi kept repeating the tongue twister to herself to try and take her mind off the fear of dropping one of the swim balls.

"If she drops just one, she's out!" Cypress said to Julie, who was watching worriedly from the wings. The gloating Cypress and La Cona looked like two vultures anticipating some poor creature's demise.

"She won't drop a single one!" snapped Julie, defending her sister.

Hovering around the water fountain, all the gingerbread make-over boys watched the monitor. They were taking bets on whether or not Jodi would be able to pull it off. Jose Éclair couldn't control his admiration for her. "I love it, love it, love it! This Jodi Needles is a maverick of style!"

Gritting her teeth while displaying her best pageant smile, Jodi had made it to the X marked on the stage floor.

"Now," Jodi commanded under her breath. The little fish instinctively reacted by swimming in fast circles, confirming what everyone in the audience had thus far been unable to detect. "Those are real fish!" There was the sound of thunderous applause followed by the blinding flash of hundreds of cameras.

Then, in an unprecedented move, Jodi stepped closer to the judges, smiling, as they were encouraged by her eyes to remove a swim trim ball from one of her limbs. In turn, Limon, Carmella and Candy each claimed a little mini fishbowl keepsake. Everyone in the house cheered. Jodi had done it again, and with originality.

Phew! She thought. *Three less balls to have to carry back.*

"She cheated!" shouted La Cona. "This isn't fair."

"No she didn't. My sister didn't say a word. It's not her fault they each took a fish ball. So if you wanna blame someone, why don't you go blame the stupid candy judges, and just see how far that gets ya!"

"Oh my!" remarked La Cona. Her bark bites had inflamed all her allergies. Up until now she had kept it to herself. But the itching and yellow needles were starting. "Not now, I have to go on," she pleaded.

Running to her aid, Jose Éclair had the perfect solution. "Trust me," he said, "I know this will work. You will be the next showstopper."

"And concluding swim balls, once again Miss Pinesky." Iza Miz-rooter and the rest of the watchers had begun to look forward to this "Who tops who?" game between Jodi and La Cona. And once again, they were not disappointed. Standing on her mark holding a large Japanese parasol, Redda's granddaughter had been sprayed from head to toe with pink flocking spray by Jose Éclair. Her swim balls, bright silver and yellow with purple glitter spots, were scattered everywhere. Two larger purple balls defined her bathing top, and two slightly larger balls had been placed both in the front and in the back at her bikini line. The pink flocking spray had worked. Her itching was gone, and so, too, any hint of yellow needles.

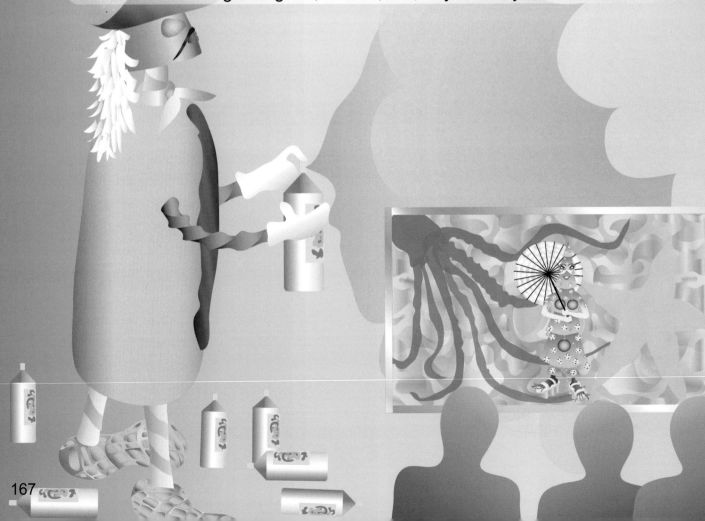

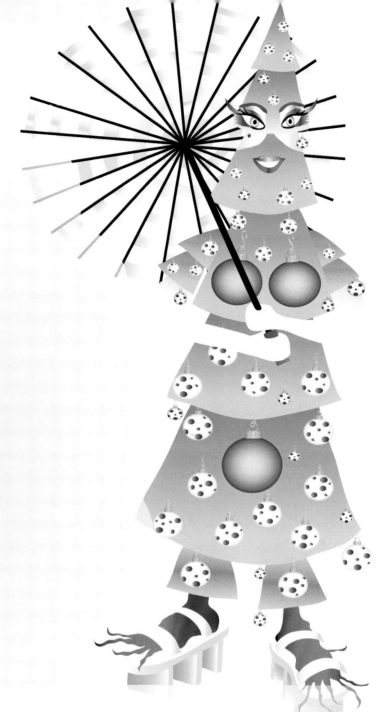

The at-home viewers had thought they'd seen everything up until this moment. "A pink Christmas Eve tree? What would be next? Perhaps gold, silver, or possibly even white? How bizarre! What had the world of Christmas tree fashions come to?"

For once in her life, Redda, still seated in the balcony, was speechless.

"Let's have a big round of candy-clap applause for our lovely green, and now, pink things," said Freddie into the cameras.

"And out to commercial." The director was all a-yammer. "We should have come to this little town years ago," he said. "These Gingertown folk will do practically anything for attention."

With not an ounce of strength left, Jodi collapsed backstage from all the water weight. *Smash! Smash! Smash!* In a flash, puddles of water, broken glass, and raspberry-red gummy-guppies lay everywhere.

The frightened, squiggly little fish flipped and flopped, trying to find water. First the stage manager, not seeing a little red gummy-guppy, took a step and... *whoosh!* He slipped and fell flat on his shortcake bottom. Then a gingerbread beauty boy consultant, who was carrying a high-topped wig creation, went gooshing and slipping on a flipping red gummy, too. Landing in a pile of costumes, the backstage candy cane helper was entangled in yards and yards of golden tree garland. For many brutal backstage minutes, it was nothing but screams and slips to the left or to the right. Every which way the red raspberry guppies flipped, a backstage contestant or helper slipped and fell.

And it was at this moment that, outside the dressing room where the more famous entertainers prepared for their entrances, someone was plotting to bring even more chaos to the event. Few ever got a glimpse of this lavishly decorated suite made of mauve marshmallow treats. The peanut brittle door was delicately carved, and fitted with a golden brass handle. The door to this very special room had a lock on it. And at present, the key to that lock was being turned by the mysterious gloved hand. Not a single slipping or sliding person took notice. The white-gloved naysayer had struck again.

"Anybody there?" said the one and only Arbra Treesand from inside the mauve marshmallow deluxe dressing room. "Guess not." Miss Treesand was tonight's special guest. Surrounded by candy bouquets and presents from adoring fans and crewmembers, she sat making a last minute check of her needled coiffure and makeup. "Good! Time to be gorgeous!" she said to herself in the mirror, and she made her way towards the door. "Hey! It's locked. Now why on earth would the door be locked?" She tapped on the door lightly, not wanting to break her perfectly painted extra, extra, extra long needled superstar fingernails. "Help? Somebody help!"

Jose Éclair, realizing that his special celebrity guest friend was about to miss her entrance, hurried to get her. "Forty-five seconds 'til air, somebody get Miss Treesand. She's on. Augh!" Falling victim to one of the hopping wet little fish, Jose Éclair also slipped out of sight, and right into the trash.

"Why is this happening to me? Help! Let me out! I'm a big star. I can't be expected to unlock this door myself. My nails are too long!" squealed Arbra.

"Now before we slide into home plate for the conclusion of the show, we have a surprise guest performer making a rare television appearance. I, Freddie Molasses, am so very proud to be standing on the same stage with… Miss Arbra Treesand!"

The red applause lights blinked. "Where is she?" The director out in the control booth was counting the seconds, waiting nervously.

Ms. Hemlock could feel bad luck falling upon her like dominos. From all her years of pageants, she knew that once accidents started to happen, more would surely follow.

"I have to get a firm grip on matters," she said aloud to no one in particular. "Where is she? Why do these big stars always act like this? We need somebody funny and we need them fast. Someone who can sing!" Getting caught up in the panic, Ms. Hemlock continued talking aloud to herself. "Maybe this show is a runaway train. Look, little fishes and puddles of water are everywhere. People are running all about. I'm losing control!"

Jiggling wildly while trying unsuccessfully to turn the inside lock without breaking her unbelievably luxurious extra, extra, extra long diva needle-nails, Miss Treesand finally decided there was only one way to get out. She had to try to unlock the door herself by turning the knob while at the same time pushing the little lock switch with the back of her hand.

Meanwhile Jose Éclair, who was climbing out of the trash, had also realized that there could only be one possible reason for the mega-superstar to miss her cue - having to open the door herself. (This was a common problem for Candywood superstars.) "I will rescue you, Miss Treesand!" he shouted.

Down on her knees, while still trying not to mess up her needles or wrinkle her gown, the superstar tree-diva put the entire doorknob in her mouth. "Ick!" It was orange-flavored fig, a taste she happened to really hate. Arbra turned her head at a right angle, turning the knob. At the same time she pushed the little latch with the back of her hand.

At the exact moment the orange-flavored fig knob was being turned by Arbra, Jose took hold of it on the other side. She quickly pulled her mouth off the knob, but before Miss Treesand could get out of the way, the door burst open. *Smack!* The knob struck her right into the middle of her forehead. Dizzy for a moment, her eyes fluttered and she fell backwards passing out.

"Ahhh! What have I done?" cried Jose Éclair. "Arbra. Arbra wake up! Wake up!" At first he shook her, but there was no response. "What am I going to do? What am I going to do?" he shouted. Then in haste the frazzled makeover beauty expert grabbed one of the many candy floral arrangements that filled the dressing room. He yanked a bouquet out of a big vase and threw it on the floor. Desperately trying to revive her, he dumped the water from inside the vase onto Miss Treesand's roots. She opened her eyes. Fortunately, due to her hard wooden forehead, she wasn't hurt as badly as Jose had first thought.

He helped her up to her feet. "How do you feel?" inquired the eager Jose.

"Where am I?" asked the throbbing superstar. She took a single step in order to regain her focus. "Oh yeah," she muttered, "Gingertown." Like the trooper she was, Miss Treesand took a deep breath and pointed one of her extra, extra, extra long needled fingers toward the open doorway. "Onward," she commanded. "The show must go on!"

Holding her elbow for added support, Jose escorted Arbra over the threshold. Then, suddenly, "Ahhh!" *Ker-splat!* Both she and Jose slipped on two flipping wet Raspberry-Red Sweetish Gummy Fish, falling flat on their backs.

The white-gloved villain snickered, now determined more than ever to stop this pageant. The fifty fish that Jodi had dropped would soon be merely a drop in the bucket, for unbeknownst to anyone other than the backstage saboteur, buckets and buckets of gummy-guppies were about to be unleashed onto the stage. One, two, three, and… DUMP! Suddenly, hundreds of little fish flopped everywhere. Even Freddie Molasses was not immune to the slippery mess, as they began to cover almost every inch of the stage.

"What are we going to do?" Ms. Hemlock shouted.

Julie had an idea. "Do you have a long-handled squeegee? The kind used for store windows?"

Befuddled and speechless, Ms. Hemlock had no earthly idea.

Overhearing Julie's request, Mr. Crumbcake, the theater's janitor, came to the rescue, and fetched the squeegee, standing at attention like a soldier waiting for further orders.

"I know how we can clean up the stage, and keep everybody in the audience happy at the same time," persisted Julie.

"How?" asked Ms. Hemlock.

"I can tap dance."

"Tap what?"

With that last word to Ms. Hemlock, Julie slipped and slided her way onto the stage. When they saw the little tree standing onstage alone, the audience chatter stopped dead.

"What's she going to do?" asked a cookie crewmember in the television control booth.

"Just let her run with it," said the director. "These Gingertown people are all very resourceful."

Julie then addressed the audience. All of the many, many TV cameras in the Barn were now aimed right at her. "Ah, excuse me, but the big surprise guest star, Miss Treesand, who was going to sing her big hit, *Evergreen People,* uh… she got locked in her dressing room, and after she got out by turning the door knob with her big mega-star mouth, she slipped on a gummy fish and broke all of her needle-nails. They just took her to the hospital."

There was a moment of awkward silence, and then gales of laughter filled the theater. Even the orchestra was laughing.

"So I guess the most important thing to remember, no matter how big a star you are, is when you're backstage at a beauty pageant…"

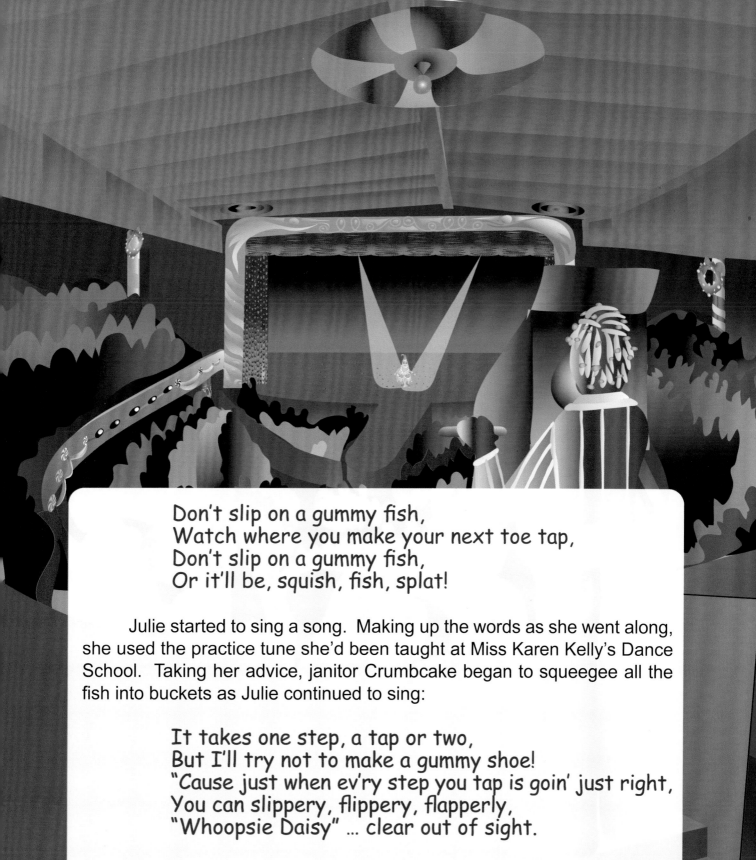

Don't slip on a gummy fish,
Watch where you make your next toe tap,
Don't slip on a gummy fish,
Or it'll be, squish, fish, splat!

Julie started to sing a song. Making up the words as she went along, she used the practice tune she'd been taught at Miss Karen Kelly's Dance School. Taking her advice, janitor Crumbcake began to squeegee all the fish into buckets as Julie continued to sing:

It takes one step, a tap or two,
But I'll try not to make a gummy shoe!
"Cause just when ev'ry step you tap is goin' just right,
You can slippery, flippery, flapperly,
"Whoopsie Daisy" ... clear out of sight.

Feeling a little more confident, Julie decided to add a few of the tap steps that she had practiced at Miss Karen's. The little fish, seeing her giant metal tap shoes coming right at them, hopped out of the way. A cameraman on the apron of the stage came in for a close-up of the little red gummies. The at-home viewing audience laughed until they fell over. "This had to be planned," they thought. "It's too funny to be an accident."

Shuffle, shuffle, shuffle, step toe shuffle
Fishy gishy slide, Fishy ishy glide.

Julie's charming little song was winning over the skeptical live audience. She told them, "Ask anyone who's ever been backstage at a beauty pageant, and they'll all say the same thing."

If your tap a, tap a, tap,
Is a tap a squish splat!

A comic close up of a gummy fish, in bug-eyed horror as it was about to be stepped on, appeared on all the monitors. Unfortunately, it got flattened by the bottom of Julie's tap shoe.

Don't be sad. Don't be blue.
Just scrape all the fish ick off your shoe

By now, the majority of the slippery fish had been squeegeed up by the janitor. The few left on the stage hopped for their little lives toward the bucket on their own initiative.

And flap heel toe, flap ball-change,
Hop toe pivot again.

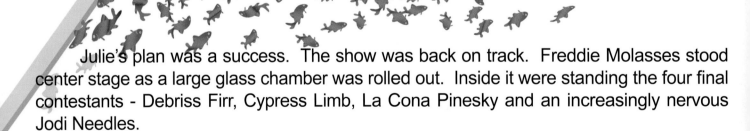

Julie's plan was a success. The show was back on track. Freddie Molasses stood center stage as a large glass chamber was rolled out. Inside it were standing the four final contestants - Debriss Firr, Cypress Limb, La Cona Pinesky and an increasingly nervous Jodi Needles.

Freddie continued to read from the teleprompter. Inside the glass booth, the green illumination of the printed words reflected on the girls' faces. "Months earlier, a special 'You Write The Final Question' box was placed, as it always has been, in front of the Gingertown Post Office. Daily, piles and piles of prospective questions were dropped inside. But it all comes down to one. The single question that will be put to all of tonight's finalists. This final question will now be chosen at random by Gingertown's first citizen, Mayor Nutty Fluffer."

Miss Candia Hemlock's Official
Christmas Eve Pageant
Question Box

A portly fluffernutter cluster of a man came onto the stage, making a grand bow towards the audience and the cameras. At first, it seemed as though things might get derailed again. For the hand Mayor Fluffer plunged into the box of questions, swirling it round and round in order to be perfectly fair, came out with dozens of little pieces of paper stuck to his sticky marshmallow fluff fingers.

"I've always heard that these small town politicians have sticky fingers, Mr. Mayor, but this is re-stickulous!" quipped Freddie, always quick with a comic barb. The audience was in stitches. "Besides, we only have time for one question, Mr. Mayor! Ha, ha, ha, ha, ha!" The Mayor chuckled good-naturedly playing along and then held his hand up in the air right above the emcee. Freddie, taking his cue, placed his left hand over his eyes, and plucked off a single question with his right.

The four finalists in the booth, seeing the onstage antics but not being able to hear what was being said, were too nervous to laugh as they anxiously awaited the pageant's final hurdle. The Final Question Round was also the pageant's Electric Light Category with regards to dress. Completely decorated from tip to bottom, adorned with classic silver strands of tinsel and a variety of accessories, the girls glowed bright with tree lights.

Each contestant must be perfectly dressed and electrified, prepared to wear the crown if one of them should win. That was how the rules had been written by Ms. Hemlock.

Debriss had on the classic big-bulbed look, as big, screw-in light bulbs were a personal family tradition. Cypress, predictably tasteful, wore a simple strand of small, country-candle-looking lights that flickered like homemade beeswax candles. La Cona, to emphasize her shocking pink-flocked physique, at the last minute had chosen strands and strands of tiny pink bulbs with little silvered mirror tree tip accents. Jodi, following her little sister's advice, was draped in every color, size and shape bulb, with blinkers and bubble lights.

Approaching the closed glass door, Freddie Molasses was ready to start. "Is there a Miss Debriss Firr in here?"

"That's me. That's me." Debriss followed Freddie to the microphone.

The perspective from within the glass chamber was rather surreal. Waiting in complete silence, Cypress, La Cona, and Jodi could hear one another's breathing.

Staring directly into Jodi's eyes while holding her gracious pageant smile, La Cona spoke without moving her lips. "Somebody took my necklace. That was my mother's necklace. I want it back."

Following her friend's lead, Cypress' sweet visual demeanor was equally as deceptive. Facing Jodi with her sappy Kentucky grin, she also barely moved her lips as she added, "And somebody took my fuchsia feather."

"What are you looking at me for?" Jodi did not take these accusations lightly.

La Cona turned to make her point clear. "Because you are her sister."

Jodi could see Julie waving at her. She was wearing the missing props.

Freddie Molasses approached again. "Miss Limb, it's your turn."

"Good Luck!" La Cona gave Cypress a quick kiss on the cheek. As expected, a wave of camera flashes went off from the chewing gum paparazzi. The two friends both vied for attention.

Left alone in the glass chamber with La Cona, Jodi smiled pleasantly and spoke too, without moving her lips. "I think the two of you have been inhaling too much needle spray, but in your case it was probably pink flocking spray."

"If I lose, you're both going to pay." La Cona's sweet southern facade showed its true bitter core. This was what Jodi loathed, and the reason she had entered in the first place.

"What are you planning to do to us? Revoke our privileges to attend your snobby warm weather social club? What a shame that would be because, I'm dreaming of a muddy Christmas."

"Try not to drop any needles when the judges ask you the final question. I hear it runs in the family."

Luckily for La Cona, this was the middle of the pageant. Any other time and Jodi would have tied her to the back of Grampa Joe's plow and dragged her through the chocolate pudding pig slop for saying anything bad about her Grandmother. "I Love To Hate You," smiles were exchanged. The door opened. "Miss Pinesky? It's your turn."

"Oh wait." Jodi pushed La Cona's face back and kissed her on the cheek. "Good luck." The wave of flashes blinded both of them. Jodi smiled. She knew how to play the game, too.

Standing alone in complete silence, Jodi had so many courses of action to consider. *I could just blow it. I could walk out there right now and tell the whole world how I feel. This is all so crazy. Why is everyone so obsessed with dressing up evergreen trees on Christmas Eve? Does any of this really matter? And if so, why? What's the point of it all?*

The end of Chapter Thirteen

Chapter Fourteen: The Point Of It All

Looking to her right, Jodi saw Julie jumping up and down with joy. On her left, seated in the center row, Gramma and Grampa were waving light-up key chains to cheer her on.

Turning once again, she saw Brian. He was licking a broom handle.

I know how badly Julie wants me to win thought Jodi, but I know that my little sister would never cheat. It's easy to point fingers when you don't have all the facts.

Suddenly the door opened. The flood of noise and light snapped Jodi out of her meditative trance.

"You are next." Taking her hand, Freddie guided her, positioning her in front of the camera reserved for close-ups.

Standing, clenching her fingers at her side, she waited quietly.

Freddie spoke. "What does Christmas Eve mean to you?"

Jodi lifted her head. Never in her life had she felt the attention of listening ears so intensely, or that what she had to say was so important. "Christmas Eve reminds me of how much my family means to me. My mom and dad, my dear Grampa, my sweet, sweet Gramma, Brian, my cute little pest of a brother, and Julie, my truly wonderful little sister. And on this very special night, I especially want them all to know just how much I love them."

Watery eyes and sniffles of emotion revealed that Jodi's simple, heart-felt answer had touched the inner soul of everyone listening. Freddie Molasses broke the emotional spell for all. "There you have it. Our four finalists."

There was a drum roll and the envelope was handed to Freddie. "The fourth runner up and the winner of a year's supply of Fertile Root Slippers… Miss Debriss Firr!"

Freddie continued. "The third runner up and the winner of a ..."

"Stop the pageant! Stop the pageant!" Desperately out of breath, Canadia Hemlock barged onto the stage.

"Now what?!" The crew in the control van could not believe what they were seeing.

"Stop the pageant! We have a saboteur in our midst."

Was this real? Or had the pressure of live television finally cracked Canadia's pinecones?

"I know now who guppy-gummied my stage. I know who's been taking all the toilet paper out of the ladies room. I know who drew a mustache on my picture in the lobby. And I know who forced a celebrity mega superstar to put a bitter orange flavored fig doorknob into her mouth."

Suspense circled the crowd.

"Who is it?" she continued. "The janitor? The stage manager? The wig master? Perhaps Jose Éclair, the eccentric Candywood creampuff and his gingerbread beauty boys? Or maybe, Debriss Firr, the innocent happy tree that says hello to everybody. Or Colorada Spruce, the downhill ski tree champion?" Taking center stage in her newly donned role of a mystery detective, Ms. Hemlock had everyone's attention piqued. "No, there are only a handful of despicables desperate to win. La Cona Pinesky?"

Redda was incensed at the accusation.

"Or sweet little Julie Needles? She tried to steal the crown, and I caught her evil little brother licking my coffee table!"

The crowd gasped in horror.

"But, I have now uncovered incontrovertible proof that..."

"I admit it. I put a mustache on your lobby poster and took all the toilet paper out of the ladies room. I did it because I was so mad. I was supposed to be the emcee this year and I didn't get to because some sweet-talking celebrity candy clown comes to town - no offense, Mister Molasses, but you are a smooth talker."

Not at all offended, Freddie spoke. "Why of course not! No offense taken, little tree. I am unable to control my smooth-talking tongue, especially with the sweet honeys backstage."

Little Ronnie Barkwood continued. The television cameras moved in closer to capture the pent-up anger he was trying so hard to control. "Anyway, I didn't get to tell my jokes. They're all very funny jokes too. And worst of all," Ronnie turned directly to Ms. Hemlock for the conclusion of his confession, "When you asked me to de-cotton-candy-lint the back of your needles before the pageant started, I just pretended to use the cotton-candy-lint roller."

Ms. Hemlock's eye's doubled in size with anger. "You mean…?"

"Yes," answered Ronnie in a vindictive tone. "Everybody's been cotton-candy-lint-laughing behind your back."

At that, Ms. Hemlock twisted herself into a position in order to see her reflection off the glass question booth. There it was. Clusters and clusters of cotton-candy-lint. And as everyone in Gingertown knew, cotton-candy-lint build up was the ultimate fashion faux pas for evergreens. Everyone was snickering. "I am very disappointed in you Ronald, and we will deal with this embarrassing episode later, when I fire you, but you are not the villain suspected of creating a real crime wave whose proof of guilt I have in my hand. That person is none other than…" Ms. Hemlock dramatically pointed her long green arm, "You! Yes you, the least likely of all!"

Pointing directly at her suspected villain, all eyes were suddenly focused on Cypress Limb.

"I was tidying up backstage between sponsor breaks, and I ran across *this* on her dressing table." Holding up for all to see, the Pageant Lady, turned Sherlock Holmes, had a bottle in her grip.

Cypress Limb, defending herself, said, "Why that's just ordinary needle moisturizer."

Very slowly, Ms. Hemlock peeled back the label. Under it was printed, "Coconut Oil."

This was shocking to everyone. Realizing she had been discovered, Cypress backed slowly from the center of the stage toward the rear wall.

"Don't let her leave!" shouted Ms. Hemlock.

The Gingerbread beauty boys aligned themselves to prevent her escape. Being cornered, Cypress Limb had no other choice. Right then and there, for all to witness, the sweet Kentucky country bumpkin transformed herself. Slowly, blue-green-needled-looking branches, which had been tightly bound, unfurled. Lifting eight large limbs high above her head, Cypress Limb's true species was revealed. She was a palm tree!

Shoes, lace headbands, mini snowflake earrings, even backstage brownie snacks baked by Colorada Spruce's mother for a good luck, fell out onto the stage.

"My brownies!" Colorada shouted. "You heartless monster."

"Brownies schmownies! Everyone stand back!" Cypress threatened.

Prepared for her dangerous spy mission, Cypress stood on guard. This was not just any ordinary palm tree. She was a rare octopus palm. Such a tree was rumored to exist, but no one had ever seen one. Stretching tall with a silver gray-trunked face, the octopus palm's hands were at each of her unfurled palm branch tips. Eight white gloves swayed above her head ready for battle. Swinging and swiping her enormous branches, all of her disguise was tossed aside.

"Good riddance!" she exclaimed. "I will no longer be a slave to gingham and country plaid panties. Yuck!"

How clever, thought Ms. Hemlock. *Who would ever suspect an eight-handed thief?*

Shriek, shriek, shriek! The octopus palm held a shriekingly high-pitched metal whistle to her slivery green gray lips.

Slam! Slam! Slam! Bang! Crash! From every window, every emergency exit, and sliding down from ropes dropped from above, the age-old Barn theater was infiltrated.

"Treequality! Treequality! We want in!"

The Junior Leaf and their angry outside protesters had made their move.

"Is this some kind of reality theater experience? If so, I love it!" Limon Sour commented to the cameras.

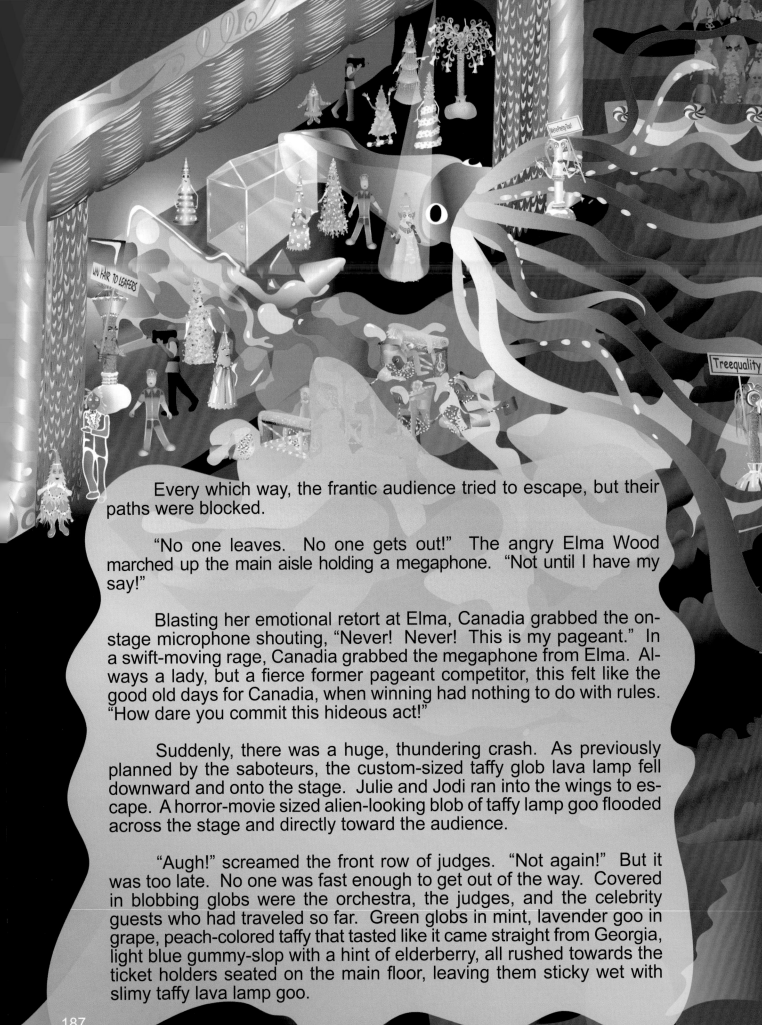

Every which way, the frantic audience tried to escape, but their paths were blocked.

"No one leaves. No one gets out!" The angry Elma Wood marched up the main aisle holding a megaphone. "Not until I have my say!"

Blasting her emotional retort at Elma, Canadia grabbed the on-stage microphone shouting, "Never! Never! This is my pageant." In a swift-moving rage, Canadia grabbed the megaphone from Elma. Always a lady, but a fierce former pageant competitor, this felt like the good old days for Canadia, when winning had nothing to do with rules. "How dare you commit this hideous act!"

Suddenly, there was a huge, thundering crash. As previously planned by the saboteurs, the custom-sized taffy glob lava lamp fell downward and onto the stage. Julie and Jodi ran into the wings to escape. A horror-movie sized alien-looking blob of taffy lamp goo flooded across the stage and directly toward the audience.

"Augh!" screamed the front row of judges. "Not again!" But it was too late. No one was fast enough to get out of the way. Covered in blobbing globs were the orchestra, the judges, and the celebrity guests who had traveled so far. Green globs in mint, lavender goo in grape, peach-colored taffy that tasted like it came straight from Georgia, light blue gummy-slop with a hint of elderberry, all rushed towards the ticket holders seated on the main floor, leaving them sticky wet with slimy taffy lava lamp goo.

Gramma, Grampa and Great Aunt Sylvia laughed. They hadn't had this much sweet-covered fun in years.

And as if that weren't enough to dampen the spirit of the pageant, Elma and her crew still had one more devious stunt up their collective Junior Leafer sleeve.

High up in the tech booth above the stage, Crabby Apples and Wanda Walnut had activated the swim segment giant starfish and giant squid. Long tentacles reached to tickle and taunt the balcony patrons who up until now had thought they were safe.

Initial laughter quickly turned to anger. "You ruined my grand-daughter's chance to win," shouted Redda Pinesky.

The tide had turned. Many in the audience began voicing their opinions. "Why don't you leaf-losers go back to Swampville where you came from? We don't want your kind here in Gingertown! You're all nothing but lazy root moochers! Get a job! The only good leaf is one that leaves us alone!"

Things were clearly getting out of hand. "We're tired of having to replant all your weedlings. They take root anywhere and everywhere, with no regard for us at all."

"Go home! Go home! Go home!"

A long-overdue fight boiled through the crowd.

The TV crew in the control booth couldn't believe what was happening. "These trees really are nuts," said the director.

Taking the live-and-on-the-air microphone from its stand, Cypress, now Octopus Palm Limb, began to address the television viewers as the fight continued in the background.

"Everyone involved with this entire event - the contestants, the hairdressers, the judges, even the audience - you all are suffering from borderline personality disorder, and with a marked propensity toward mood swings ranging from extreme and overt narcissism to multiple personality disorder."

Everyone looked up for a second speechless, "Huh?"

"You're all pathetic!" she added.

Jodi was furious. "Hey that's my speech! If anybody is going to call these pageant groupies overt narcissistic mood-swinging losers, it's going to be me! I plan on being a psychologist." Jodi attacked the Octopus Palm with a bucket of red gummy fish.

"We have to finish the pageant!" shouted Julie. "Stop fighting. Please! Please stop!" The violent turmoil had roared out of control. Julie's pleas went unheard. "Look everyone, it's almost midnight." Trying to come up with some sort of plan, Julie shook with anxiety. Then as though a light bulb went on in her head, she had an idea. She began searching for just the right person to help her. Slipping in and out between all the crazy activity, Julie managed to find who she was looking for seated behind one of the large television cameras. "Mr. Molasses. Please, you have to help me."

"Shhh. Quiet girl. I don't want any of those crazy fans to know that I'm here. This is the best place to hide whenever a live TV show turns into a reality riot. The cameramen are like neutral countries when the fighting begins."

"I need to know who won the contest. Its already two minutes past midnight. There are only eight minutes of pageant wishes left."

"How would I know?"

"You have the envelope," exclaimed Julie.

"No I don't… Oh! Maybe I do!" he said. Checking his pockets, he realized he did. "Here you go sweetie." Freddie Molasses handed the unopened envelope to Julie.

"Don't you want to know who won?"

"Frankly Child, I couldn't give a flying fudge brownie about the rest of this crazy contest."

Holding the answer in her hand, Julie didn't have time to be squeamish. Just one big rip of the envelope and… "Jodi won! She won!" Julie had known her sister could do it, and inside her heart she was so proud of her, but this was no time to celebrate. Now Julie had to find the crown before the wish time ran out.

Standing guard over the precious crown just offstage was the frail little pageant treesistant. "Stand back!" he declared in his meek voice. "No one gets the crown. Come wind or rain or snow or sleet, I have sworn to protect the Christmas Eve Pageant crown." Holding a giant candy cane as a sword, he waved it in front of himself. "Even if I did put a mustache on the lobby poster, I didn't mean it. I was mad because I had some really funny jokes, and now no one will ever hear them. Do you want to hear them?"

"Yes I'd love to hear them, but I don't have much time right now. There are only seven minutes of wishes left," pleaded Julie.

"I'm sorry, but the only tree that can wear this crown is the winner of the pageant," answered the little protector.

"My sister won. I have the judge's score right here. See? And she said I could have the crown and the wishes if she won." Julie held up the winning announcement.

The suspicious little tree glanced at it. "Hmm, I'll give you the crown if you let me tell you one joke."

Julie thought for a second then said, "Okay one joke. But I only have six minutes and thirty seconds left."

"I'll make it a fast one." Little Ronnie cleared his throat. He was so excited at the thought of someone actually listening to one of his jokes that he didn't see what was happening behind him. Brian quietly took the crown off the big blue velvet pillow on which it sat. He put it on his head and ran off laughing.

Julie yelled to him. "Brian, come back, I need that crown!"

"He's got the crown?" shouted Ronnie. "Stop him! Stop him! He's got the crown!!!"

La Cona, seeing all this, interjected. "This pageant was fixed. You and your sister cheated! I am the only one here who rightfully deserves to be the winner." La Cona ran after Brian, also determined to get hold of the crown. "That crown belongs to me, you little rootweed. Give it to me!"

Laughing as he ran, Brian enjoyed the chase. Then remembering that the crown had magical wish powers, he turned around with a gleam in his eye. Brian pointed his finger at La Cona and with a focused stare. *Ka-poof!* La Cona's roots had been planted into a big metal washtub.

"Augh!" she screamed.

Then Brian pointed to others that were chasing him and did the same. *Ka-poof, Ka-poof, Ka-poof!* Now Miss Colorada Spruce, Miss Debriss Firr, and little Ronnie Barkwood were also planted into washtubs.

"Why do these things always happen to me?" the little treesistant said, looking deflatedly at his current, planted condition.

Having escaped his chasers, Brian locked himself into the glass booth that was still positioned center stage. Once inside, he giggled as he continued to make prankish wishes. *Ka-poof!* Suddenly, fluffy snow fell magically from within the theater. *Ka-poof!* Now everyone in the theater was wearing long colorful stocking caps with bells on the tips. *Ka-poof!* Now everyone was also wearing red rubber clown noses. Then he started to point at spots inside the booth. *Ka-poof! Ka-poof! Ka-poof!* The glass chamber began filling up with Brian's Christmas gift wishes. Toys and candy instantly materialized around his little blue rubber boots.

Then, Julie was standing outside of the chamber rapping on the glass. "Brian! It's my turn. I need to make a wish. I said you could use it after I got my wish. Hurry up!! There are only about three minutes left. Please Brian."

Realizing that he had indeed made a deal with his sister earlier during the pageant - that deal being that if he behaved and if Jodi won, Julie would share her wishes with him - he smiled and said, "Alright. You can have it now." He opened the glass door to the silent chamber, but with all the toys blocking his sight, he didn't see La Cona. She had yanked her muddy roots out of the metal tub and wrapped them in the stocking caps that Brian had wished on everyone. Bells shook on her toe tips with every step. This very driven, hothouse southern beauty was also still wearing the humiliating red rubber nose that Brian had magically stuck on everyone.

"It's mine!" La Cona snatched the gold star crown off of Brian's head and put it on her own. "Now you are going to get yours, both of you, all of you!" she shouted. Then, in a feverous witching, twitching, fist-shaking wave of her limbs, La Cona gathered up all her innermost anger. Up it boiled. *Ker-plink!* Nothing. "You used up all the wishes you little brat!" she scowled. Again she focused and pointed to the two little trees. *Ker-plink.* Nothing.

"It doesn't work because you didn't win and you're a bad loser." Octopus Palm, or Cypress Limb as all had come to know her, stood tall behind La Cona. She snatched the crown off La Cona's tip-top.

"I thought you were my friend," said La Cona. "Even if you are a palm tree."

"How could anybody be friends with you? Your whole life is about you. You, you, you!" Imitating the neurotic behavior of La Cona, Octopus Palm, alias Cypress Limb, mocked, *"Oh aren't my needles lovely? My bark is as delicate as a seedling's root bottom. My eyes are a perfect shade of aqua and green mixed with golden flecks, aren't they?'* There isn't enough room in your little hothouse world for a ladybug, let alone a friend."

"Jodi, Brian, somebody, help! I need the crown before the time is up." Coming to her aid, Jodi, Brian, Ronnie Barkwood, and Ms. Hemlock all tackled the Octopus Palm to retrieve the crown. Rolling around in a ball of anger, Julie could see the second hand on the big backstage clock ticking towards the end of the wish magic.

"I have it! I have it!" yelled Jodi.

"No you don't!" exclaimed La Cona. "Wish or no wish, I still want it." And back into the pile of fighting tree limbs went Jodi, crown in hand.

Slipping out of the determined grips of both Jodi and La Cona, the golden tiara finally fell to the floor. Julie's eyes opened wide with joy. She reached for the crown, which was only inches from her mitten-covered fingers. Then without warning, a large rooted foot of sizable strength stamped down hard, flattening the five-pointed star into a pile of twisted metal and broken rhinestones. Julie looked up to see Elma Wood and Silvera Birch. Pleased with the destruction of the winter pageant symbol, the two angry leaf ladies cheered in victory.

Julie picked up the mangled little star and placed it on her head. It was too late. All the time had run out, as had all the magic that went with the damaged crown. Taking deep breaths and trying with all her might not to cry, her lower lip still quivered uncontrollably. The saddest part of all was that no one there even knew that Julie's last chance to be home for Christmas, back in the world she came from, back with those she had taken for granted and now missed so desperately, had just passed her by.

The end of Chapter Fourteen

Chapter Fifteen: The Magic Doesn't Last Forever

Sorrow and heartbreak filled Julie's inner soul. Then she thought to herself, If this crazy world is the one that I'm going to be living in, then something has to be done to teach everyone here the true spirit of Christmas.

Having reached her limit with such childish behavior, Julie's sorrow turned into little girl rage. She decided that the time had come to do something drastic. She picked up two microphones and put them together in front of one of the large stage speakers. The loud, deafening sound of immense feedback pierced and rattled the crowd, quaking the old Barn Theater, shaking all the red rubber clown noses off of everyone. The noses went bouncing in all directions. Then she put both microphones up to her lips and shouted:

"Everybody stop!" Her voice resonated even outside, all the way to the Sequoia Red Fountain, cracking the layers of winter's frozen ice. The town stopped dead.

"I've got something to say. You may have heard it before, from your mother or on the news, but it needs to be said again and again and again."

The racing hearts of the fist-shaking mob began to hasten.

"It's not supposed to be like this, not in July, October, March, April or even May."

Ashamed of their outrageous conduct, many of the audience members nodded in agreement.

"If I had one great big wish, it would be for everybody to share a great big world-wide mistletoe kiss. Think of all the things we could be doing instead of fighting. Especially on Christmas Eve!"

The TV technicians, feeling embarrassed at so thoroughly enjoying these angry antics, were deeply moved by Julie's statement. "Hey, the kid's right, let's help her out." Utilizing their master control station, the technicians began to make adjustments and flick switches. The main floor of the theater softened, enveloped in a more soothing light. A spotlight was activated, and the hard-candy mirror ball lowered into place. The members of the orchestra, having removed the bulk of the sticky mess that had covered their music stands and instruments, took a cue from the control booth and accompanied Julie's plea.

Transcribing every heartfelt thought, the broadcast computer technician added his own special touch from the keyboard. At home, the television viewers read Julie's word's along the bottom of their screens as she sang her song of Christmas love.

Why can't everybody get along?
Why not today of all days?
It's not supposed to be like this.
We should be sharing in a great big kiss!

Why can't everybody get along?
Why not today of all days?

As the mood changed, candy couples and tree couples slow-danced across the main floor. Christmas spirit was building again.

Especially on Christmas Eve...

Images of glob-covered audience members with microphones put up to their chins for comments appeared on the air. "I should be standing in long lines at the mall looking for last-minute bargains right now," said one of the slow- dancers to the camera.

"We should be stuffing our kid's stockings with glow in the dark pencils and musical tooth brushes," commented another couple.

"And I should be at home scraping price tags off cheap 99¢ gifts before I wrap them... and heating up leftover frozen pizza," added Tee Zee Anne who some how got mixed into the rioting shuffle.

Julie's big band styled song ended with one last thought-provoking lyric.

What ever happened... to Christmas love?

Julie had said and sang all she could. There was nothing left to do.

Seizing the moment, Oakanna, as usual, had to have the last word. Pointing to Canadia Hemlock, she said, spitefully, "It's all her fault."

"Oh, go suck an acorn!" retorted the Pageant Lady.

Before this little verbal dispute had a chance to grow into a war of principles, Julie spoke up. "I have an idea!"

Everyone listened.

"But it won't work unless everybody agrees."

The consensus was unanimous! After all, she had managed to save the pageant during the red gummy fish fiasco.

Marching down Baker's way past the Petit Four Pet Store and the Pageant Office, a proud gingerbread-man and candy-cane color guard led the parade. It was bright and early the next morning. A light flurry of snow sprinkled the well-wishers that stood along the parade route.

The pageant's swim-trim starfish had been redesigned, and was now filled with helium and painted bright gold. The beauty boy makeover crew was leading the starfish, now a giant air balloon, by long ropes as it floated along Baker's Way. Following behind the enormous balloon was Jose Éclair, waving and tossing gifts from his oversized trim sack. Root-tooting whistlers and party noisemakers celebrated each and every step.

"Hello! I am Freddie Molasses, your Master of Parade Ceremonies, here in Gingertown on this wonderful Christmas morning."

"And I am also so happy to be here, too." Seated next to Freddie and helping host the parade was the charming Arbra Treesand. Her extra, extra, extra long needle-nails had been bandaged, and the day before's misfortune had not affected her happy demeanor. "What a funny girlish turn of events on this very clear day. Why you can almost see for-ever and ever in this frosting covered mountain town. The new standard of mirrored beauty for this pageant truly does have two tree faces, both conifer and deciduous."

"And this is Graham Jelly Roll reporting down on street level here at Baker's Way bringing you this first-ever Gingertown Christmas Day Parade. I see one of the pageant contestants from last night riding on an approaching float. I'll see if I can get a word from her."

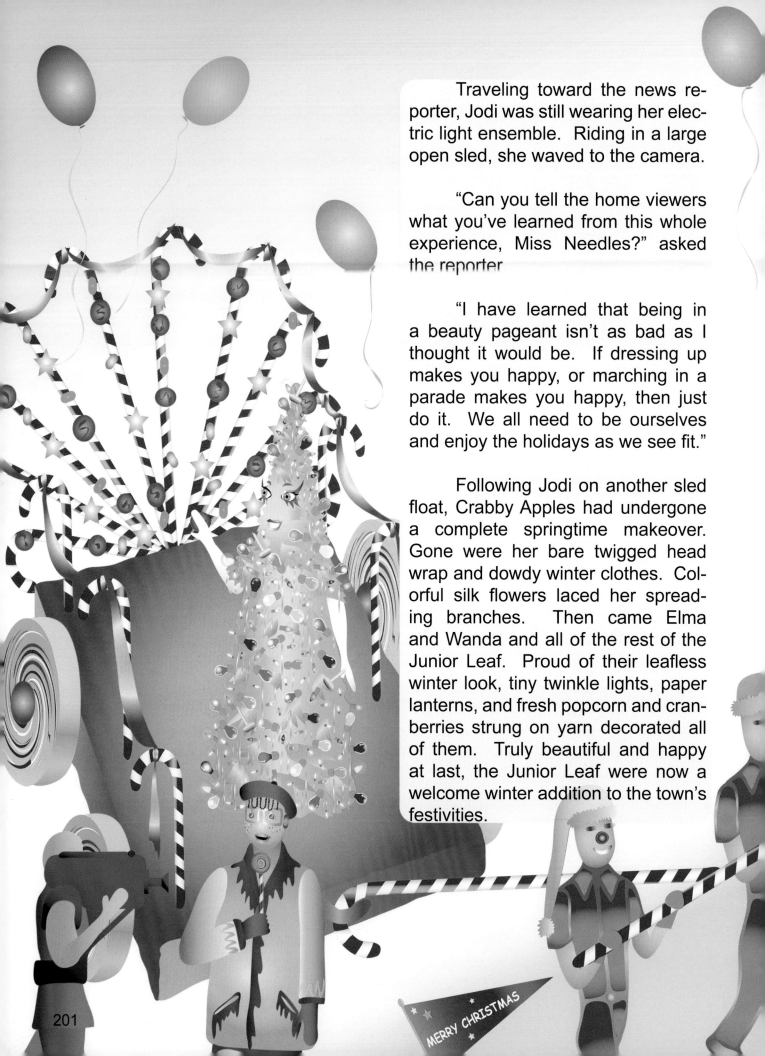

Traveling toward the news reporter, Jodi was still wearing her electric light ensemble. Riding in a large open sled, she waved to the camera.

"Can you tell the home viewers what you've learned from this whole experience, Miss Needles?" asked the reporter.

"I have learned that being in a beauty pageant isn't as bad as I thought it would be. If dressing up makes you happy, or marching in a parade makes you happy, then just do it. We all need to be ourselves and enjoy the holidays as we see fit."

Following Jodi on another sled float, Crabby Apples had undergone a complete springtime makeover. Gone were her bare twigged head wrap and dowdy winter clothes. Colorful silk flowers laced her spreading branches. Then came Elma and Wanda and all of the rest of the Junior Leaf. Proud of their leafless winter look, tiny twinkle lights, paper lanterns, and fresh popcorn and cranberries strung on yarn decorated all of them. Truly beautiful and happy at last, the Junior Leaf were now a welcome winter addition to the town's festivities.

MERRY CHRISTMAS

Standing next to Ida Mae, her long time friend Redda, also riding the glamorous sled float, displayed her new holiday fashion splurge. She had flocked herself in cotton candy pink from top to bottom. Laughing while holding La Cona's equally sprayed pink hand, Redda shouted, "I had an itch! And you're only young once, right?"

Riding last, hitched to the back of the sled boat, Cypress Limb, now in her rare truly tropical octopus palm form, wearing a grass skirt and candy-lei necklaces, did the Holiday Hula for all with pride. Protected from the cold winter winds, she blew kisses from within the converted glass pageant question chamber.

Positioned at Julie's side, Ms. Hemlock bent lower to speak. "How do you feel about ten minutes of magic wishes?"

"Me?" Julie was surprised at this offer. "I thought the wishing crown was broken."

"Correct. That little cutie of a star was officially trash-ola. That was of course until Ronald stayed up all night with the aid of Sticky Sap Cola glue and repaired it," explained Canadia. "A little paint, a few more beads here and there and look, it's as good as new."

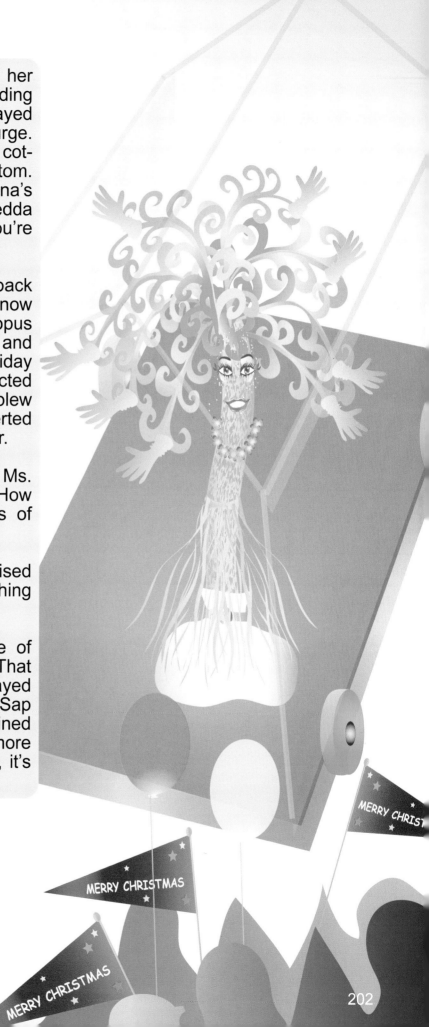

MERRY CHRIST

MERRY CHRISTMAS

MERRY CHRISTMAS

MERRY CHRI

Ronnie held up the velvet blue pillow on which the crown sat. It was as pretty as ever.

Canadia picked up the newly repaired five pointed star tiara. She spoke. "The Gingertown Christmas Eve Pageant wishing crown was my very first wishing crown, and now I want to make it yours."

Holding up the megaphone, which had been previously used by the protestors the night before, Canadia made a proclamation of grand distinction. "For having the generous insight to include everyone in the first ever Gingertown Christmas Day Parade, I, Canadia Hemlock, or the Pageant Lady as most of the town folk call me, officially crown you, Julie Needles, the first Little Miss Christmas Day Parade Princess."

Everyone Cheered.

Canadia placed the star tiara on Julie's tree top tip. The extra added baubles made it even more spectacular. Aurora Borealis rainbow cut crystals were used to fill in all the little cracks and glue spots. It cast a glow of true royalty. "Start wishing kid. Remember, the magic doesn't last forever."

Seated on her large parade throne, Julie lifted her limbs high. "I believe that all trees deserve to wear a crown on Christmas Day. That will be my first wish." Then woosh! Instantly hundreds of glimmering crowns and star tiaras materialized on the tops of all the trees in Gingertown. And Julie had made sure that her wish included all the trees, evergreens and the Leafers alike.

Gramma had a gold star with ruby red sparkles. Grampa wore a handsome silver star burst with blue sparkles. Brian had a little purple star, and Jodi's was covered in elegant pearl beads.

Tears of joy fell from both La Cona's and Redda's eyes as they too were crowned in winning style.

Julie felt that the ladies of the Junior Leaf deserved a little extra something to help make up for all the years of winter neglect that they had endured. She swirled her fingers towards them. Magically all of the Junior Leafers' bare winter branches were covered with green crystals. Never before had the leaf ladies felt more beautiful. The magic green crystal leaves added a touch of the dramatic to their already splendidly decorated parade attire.

"Everyone here also deserves a present. I wish one for everyone in Gingertown," she declared. Suddenly all of the colorful candy people that were lining the parade route, along with the trees, the snow people and the visiting celebrities, felt a magical tingle as Julie's unique taste in holiday gifts materialized. What she gave everyone were necklaces made of popcorn, peanuts, cranberries and marshmallows. Hanging off each festive necklace was a small wrapped gift box, and inside each little box was a wonderful little keepsake.

Julie turned to Ms. Hemlock all-aglow. "Thank you, thank you, thank you! I wish for you the most beautiful golden tree trimmings ever!"

Instantly, the Pageant Lady was adorned with luxurious golden baubles.

Satisfied that she had done her best to share her wishes of good cheer with all, Julie closed her eyes. A melting inner core of emotions quivered inside. She was finally going to get her wish. Whirls and swirls of magical stars, snowflakes and colors raced in her mind. Faster and faster, until… she opened her eyes.

She looked at her hands. They were normal again! She had two feet with real toes and two ears that she tugged on to make sure she was not in the midst of some deep, sleepy dream. "I'm real! I'm a girl again! Gramma! Grampa! Christmas morning - it's here!" Julie jumped out of bed and ran down the big front hall stairs.

"Surprise!" cheered everyone as she entered the main parlor.

"While you were sleeping the entire family secretly decorated the tree you picked out with the beautiful decorations you made." Gramma put her arm around Julie. "So what do you think of it?"

"It's the prettiest tree ever," announced Julie.

Gathered in the living room sipping hot chocolate and eating bite-sized breakfast gingerbread men, Julie and her family were all back to normal.

Standing for a moment, feeling a little embarrassed about the way she had behaved earlier, Julie walked over to where Gramma and Grampa were sitting.

206

"I'm sorry for acting like a big brat. I love it here. You didn't ruin Christmas. I almost did." They both hugged her in a big three-way bear-clump hug. Knowing all was well, Julie just smiled with joy at all the wrapped gifts scattered under the tree.

"Open your present. It's from me and Jodi." Brian handed Julie a holiday wrapped box. Christmas day - with all of it's blinking and twinkling lights and Christmas cards lined up on the mantle, with gift booties that were hanging filled with fresh frosted treats and the Gingertown village that Gramma had so carefully baked - was most definitely here.

"A Talking Teresa doll!" Julie's gift wish had not been forgotten.

Julie pushed the talking doll's button. It spoke. "Let's play beauty pageant." Julie laughed.

"Look, Julie. One more gift! It's from me and Grampa." Brian handed Julie a little box. "I wrapped it."

And it looked like the wrapping of an ambitious little brother, thought Julie. The box had been wrapped in a page from an old comic book, with a striped sneaker shoelace for a ribbon. It made Julie laugh.

"Open it," Brian said with an excited smile.

Julie pulled the tied bow and removed the comics to discover a little tin throat-lozenge box. She lifted the metal lid and inside was yet another little bundle. Whatever it was, it had almost an entire roll of bath tissue wrapped around it. Julie unwound and unwound and unwound until it seemed that there would be nothing inside but a practical joke. Then to her surprise…

"My penny! How did you get it? Grampa!" She ran over to hug him.

Grampa laughed. "Oh, you wouldn't believe it if I told you."

"Yes I would." Julie hugged him again.

"First I thought…'Hmm… maybe Tiger Lily could…'"

"I thought the same thing," exclaimed Julie.

The entire family gathered around his overstuffed armchair as Grampa shared the tale of how he rescued the carnival penny from the well. "Do you all remember that electric beachcomber magnet that I bought a long time ago? You know, that blue thing with the crazy bike handles. It's been lying up on the shelf in the tool shed for years. Well I thought if I got a strong rope and…"

As Julie listened, all of her incredible Gingertown experiences were still racing through her mind - talking candy people, sugar-coated buildings, barreling down a mine shaft propelled by roller-skating topiary trees, eating blue frosting party-cake sandwiches at the Wedding Cake Café, singing and tap squishy-fish dancing in front of hundreds of crazy cookie-people at the Barn Theater, and a magical parade with waving elm trees decorated in paper lanterns and sparkling green crystal covered branches. Had she really convinced them all to get along? Had any of it been real, or had it been the fanciful imaginings of a little girl with a lost wishing-well penny?

"So now that Grampa got your penny back, what are you going to wish for?" asked Gramma.

"I think I've had enough magical wishes," said Julie. "At least for a while."

Then, something made Julie look at the beautiful balsa pine that dominated the parlor. This graceful tree, covered top to bottom with homemade decorations, seemed strangely familiar somehow. As she gazed upward, an evergreen face suddenly appeared amongst the branches. It was the clown lady in the circus. She was really there in the tree, really licking a sucker, and really wearing a pointy green witches' hat. Julie winked and nodded, and for one magical moment the familiar face smiled and winked back at her.

The holiday wish, with a frozen winter twist, was finally complete.

The End

Author's Notes

Many things in Gingertown were directly inspired by my childhood memories – Cutting down fresh Christmas trees; Frosting cut out cookies at Nana's; Walking to "Murphy's" the local five and dime store to purchase little gifts that kids could afford to buy; Crafting new decorations from old broken ones; and Lying on my mother's brand new, blue-green, wall to wall carpeted floor while watching Christmas specials on a three channel black and white television.

While there was certainly plenty of snow growing up in the village of Lancaster, New York, the wide spread image of the traditional Victorian Christmas, though charming, is not the holiday I knew. It was my goal in writing and illustrating Gingertown to create a fantasy rooted in the more modern sense of family and the experiences that I so fondly remember.

For additional e-book, audio book, general product development, and purchasing information, go to GINGERTOWN.COM

A special note of gratitude to the following individuals whose contributions have been invaluable; Mark Janas, Jim Pluskota, Sylvia Gillam, Kevin Gillam, Kimberly Dawn Neumann, Dennis Mack, and Jodi Buckley.

Regardless of your own individual talents, drive, dedication and determination, it still takes the power of others to bring your vision to life.

An additional thank you to yet more friends, Paul Vasquez, Mariann Moery, Julie Reyburn, Danny Whitman, James Eden, Anto & Ciaria Nolan, and Andy Seaman.